THE OUTCASTS
OF POKER FLAT

The Outcasts of Poker Flat

Including
Luck of Roaring Camp
and Other Selected Stories

By
BRET HARTE

AMEREON HOUSE

Copyright   1982
Amereon House

Library of Congress Catalog Card Number 82-70024
International Standard Book Number 0-88411-592-5

To order, contact:
AMEREON HOUSE
Box 1200
Mattituck, New York 11952

Printed in the United States of America by
The Mad Printers of Mattituck

CONTENTS

THE OUTCASTS OF
POKER FLAT

As Mr. John Oakhurst, gambler, stepped into
the main street of Poker Flat on the morning of the
23d of November, 1850, he was conscious of a change
in its moral atmosphere since the preceding night. Two
or three men, conversing earnestly together, ceased as
he approached, and exchanged significant glances.
There was a Sabbath lull in the air, which, in a settlement unused to Sabbath influences, looked ominous.

Mr. Oakhurst's calm, handsome face betrayed small
concern in these indications. Whether he was conscious of any predisposing cause was another question. "I reckon they're after somebody," he reflected;
"likely it's me." He returned to his pocket the handkerchief with which he had been whipping away the red
dust of Poker Flat from his neat boots, and quietly discharged his mind of any further conjecture.

In point of fact, Poker Flat was "after somebody."
It had lately suffered the loss of several thousand dollars, two valuable horses, and a prominent citizen. It
was experiencing a spasm of virtuous reaction, quite as
lawless and ungovernable as any of the acts that had
provoked it. A secret committee had determined to

rid the town of all improper persons. This was done permanently in regard to two men who were then hanging from the boughs of a sycamore in the gulch, and temporarily in the banishment of certain other objectionable characters. I regret to say that some of these were ladies. It is but due to the sex, however, to state that their impropriety was professional, and it was only in such easily established standards of evil that Poker Flat ventured to sit in judgment.

Mr. Oakhurst was right in supposing that he was included in this category. A few of the committee had urged hanging him as a possible example and a sure method of reimbursing themselves from his pockets of the sums he had won from them. "It's agin justice," said Jim Wheeler, "to let this yer young man from Roaring Camp—an entire stranger—carry away our money." But a crude sentiment of equity residing in the breasts of those who had been fortunate enough to win from Mr. Oakhurst overruled this narrower local prejudice.

Mr. Oakhurst received his sentence with philosophic calmness, none the less coolly that he was aware of the hesitation of his judges. He was too much of a gambler not to accept fate. With him life was at best an uncertain game, and he recognized the usual percentage in favor of the dealer.

A body of armed men accompanied the deported wickedness of Poker Flat to the outskirts of the settlement. Besides Mr. Oakhurst, who was known to be a coolly desperate man, and for whose intimidation the armed escort was intended, the expatriated party consisted of a young woman familiarly known as "The Duchess"; another who had won the title of

"Mother Shipton"; and "Uncle Billy," a suspected sluice-robber and confirmed drunkard. The cavalcade provoked no comments from the spectators, nor was any word uttered by the escort. Only when the gulch which marked the uttermost limit of Poker Flat was reached, the leader spoke briefly and to the point. The exiles were forbidden to return at the peril of their lives.

As the escort disappeared, their pent-up feelings found vent in a few hysterical tears from the Duchess some bad language from Mother Shipton, and a Parthian volley of expletives from Uncle Billy. The philosophic Oakhurst alone remained silent. He listened calmly to Mother Shipton's desire to cut somebody's heart out, to the repeated statements of the Duchess that she would die in the road, and to the alarming oaths that seemed to be bumped out of Uncle Billy as he rode forward. With the easy good humor characteristic of his class, he insisted upon exchanging his own riding-horse, "Five-Spot," for the sorry mule which the Duchess rode. But even this act did not draw the party into any closer sympathy. The young woman readjusted her somewhat draggled plumes with a feeble, faded coquetry; Mother Shipton eyed the possessor of "Five-Spot" with malevolence, and Uncle Billy included the whole party in one sweeping anathema.

The road to Sandy Bar—a camp that, not having as yet experienced the regenerating influences of Poker Flat, consequently seemed to offer some invitation to the emigrants—lay over a steep mountain range. It was distant a day's severe travel. In that advanced season the party soon passed out of the moist, temperate regions of the foothills into the dry, cold, bracing air of the Sierras. The trail was narrow and difficult. At noon the Duchess, rolling out of her saddle upon the ground, declared her intention of going no farther, and the party halted.

The spot was singularly wild and impressive. A wooded amphitheatre, surrounded on three sides by precipitous cliffs of naked granite, sloped gently toward the crest of another precipice that overlooked the valley. It was, undoubtedly, the most suitable spot for a camp, had camping been advisable. But Mr. Oakhurst knew that scarcely half the journey to Sandy Bar was accomplished, and the party were not equipped or provisioned for delay. This fact he pointed out to his companions curtly, with a philosophic commentary on the folly of "throwing up their hand before the game was played out." But they were furnished with liquor, which in this emergency stood them in place of food, fuel, rest, and prescience. In spite of his remonstrances, it was not long before they were more or less under its influence. Uncle Billy passed rapidly from a bellicose state into one of stupor, the Duchess became maudlin, and Mother Shipton snored. Mr. Oakhurst alone remained erect, leaning against a rock, calmly surveying them.

Mr. Oakhurst did not drink. It interfered with a profession which required coolness, impassiveness, and presence of mind, and in his own language, he "couldn't afford it." As he gazed at his recumbent fellow exiles, the loneliness begotten of his pariah trade, his habits of life, his very vices, for the first time seriously oppressed him. He bestirred himself in dusting his black clothes, washing his hands and face, and other acts characteristic of his studiously neat habits, and for a moment forgot his annoyance. The thought of deserting his weaker and more pitiable companions never perhaps occurred to him. Yet he could not help feeling the want of that excitement which, singularly enough, was most conducive to that calm equanimity for which he was notorious. He looked at the gloomy walls that rose a thousand feet sheer above the circling pines around him, at the sky ominously clouded, at the valley below, already deepening into shadow; and doing so, suddenly he heard his own name called.

A horseman slowly ascended the trail. In the fresh, open face of the newcomer Mr. Oakhurst recognized Tom Simson, otherwise known as "The Innocent," of Sandy Bar. He had met him some months before over a "little game," and had, with perfect equanimity, won the entire fortune—amounting to some forty dollars—of that guileless youth. After the game was finished, Mr. Oakhurst drew the youthful speculator behind the door and thus addressed him: "Tommy, you're a good little man, but you can't gamble worth a cent. Don't try it over again." He then handed him his money back, pushed him gently from the room, and so made a devoted slave of Tom Simson.

There was a remembrance of this in his boyish and enthusiastic greeting of Mr. Oakhurst. He had started, he said, to go to Poker Flat to seek his fortune. "Alone?" No, not exactly alone; in fact (a giggle), he had run away with Piney Woods. Didn't Mr. Oakhurst remember Piney? She that used to wait on the table at the Temperance House? They had been engaged a long time, but old Jake Woods had objected, and so they had run away, and were going to Poker Flat to be married, and here they were. And they were tired out, and how lucky it was they had found a place to camp, and company. All this the Innocent delivered rapidly, while Piney, a stout, comely damsel of fifteen, emerged from behind the pine tree, where she had been blushing unseen, and rode to the side of her lover.

Mr. Oakhurst seldom troubled himself with sentiment, still less with propriety; but he had a vague idea that the situation was not fortunate. He retained, however, his presence of mind sufficiently to kick Uncle Billy, who was about to say something, and Uncle Billy was sober enough to recognize in Mr. Oakhurst's kick a superior power that would not bear trifling. He then endeavored to dissuade Tom Simson from delaying further, but in vain. He even pointed out the fact that there was no provision, nor means of making a camp. But, unluckily, the Innocent met this objection by assuring the party that he was provided with an extra mule loaded with provisions, and by the discovery of a rude attempt at a log house near the trail. "Piney can stay with Mrs. Oakhurst," said the Innocent, pointing to the Duchess, "and I can shift for myself."

Nothing but Mr. Oakhurst's admonishing foot saved Uncle Billy from bursting into a roar of laughter. As it was, he felt compelled to retire up the canyon until he could recover his gravity. There he confided the joke to the tall pine trees, with many slaps of his leg, contortions of his face, and the usual profanity. But when he returned to the party, he found them seated by a fire—for the air had grown strangely chill and the sky overcast—in apparently amicable conversation. Piney was actually talking in an impulsive girlish fashion to the Duchess, who was listening with an interest and animation she had not shown for many days. The Innocent was holding forth, apparently with equal effect, to Mr. Oakhurst and Mother Shipton, who was actually relaxing into amiability. "Is this yer a d—d picnic?" said Uncle Billy, with inward scorn, as he surveyed the sylvan group, the glancing firelight, and the tethered animals in the foreground. Suddenly an idea mingled with the alcoholic fumes that disturbed his brain. It was apparently of a jocular nature, for he felt impelled to slap his leg again and cram his fist into his mouth.

As the shadows crept slowly up the mountain, a slight breeze rocked the tops of the pine trees and moaned through their long and gloomy aisles. The ruined cabin, patched and covered with pine boughs, was set apart for the ladies. As the lovers parted, they unaffectedly exchanged a kiss, so honest and sincere that it might have been heard above the swaying pines. The frail Duchess and the malevolent Mother Shipton were probably too stunned to remark upon this last evidence of simplicity, and so turned without a word to the hut. The fire was replenished, the men lay down before the door, and in a few minutes were asleep.

Mr. Oakhurst was a light sleeper. Toward morning he awoke benumbed and cold. As he stirred the dying fire, the wind, which was now blowing strongly, brought to his cheek that which caused the blood to leave it—snow!

He started to his feet with the intention of awakening the sleepers, for there was no time to lose. But turning to where Uncle Billy had been lying, he found him gone. A suspicion leaped to his brain, and a curse to his lips. He ran to the spot where the mules had been tethered—they were no longer there. The tracks were already rapidly disappearing in the snow.

The momentary excitement brought Mr. Oakhurst back to the fire with his usual calm. He did not waken the sleepers. The Innocent slumbered peacefully, with a smile on his good-humored, freckled face; the virgin Piney slept beside her frailer sisters as sweetly as though attended by celestial guardians; and Mr. Oakhurst, drawing his blanket over his shoulders, stroked his mustaches and waited for the dawn. It came slowly in a whirling mist of snowflakes that dazzled and confused the eye. What could be seen of the landscape appeared magically changed. He looked over the valley, and summed up the present and future in two words, "Snowed in!"

A careful inventory of the provisions, which, fortunately for the party, had been stored within the hut, and so escaped the felonious fingers of Uncle Billy, disclosed the fact that with care and prudence they might last ten days longer. "That is," said Mr. Oakhurst *sotto voce* to the Innocent, "if you're willing to board us. If you ain't—and perhaps you'd better not—you can wait till Uncle Billy gets back with provisions." For some occult reason, Mr. Oakhurst could not bring himself to disclose Uncle Billy's rascality, and so offered the hypothesis that he had wandered from the camp and had accidentally stampeded the animals. He dropped a warning to the Duchess and Mother Shipton, who of course knew the facts of their associate's defection. "They'll find out the truth about us *all* when they find out anything," he added significantly, "and there's no good frightening them now."

Tom Simson not only put all his worldly store at the disposal of Mr. Oakhurst, but seemed to enjoy the prospect of their enforced seclusion. "We'll have a good camp for a week, and then the snow'll melt, and we'll all go back together." The cheerful gayety of the young man and Mr. Oakhurst's calm infected the others. The Innocent, with the aid of pine boughs, extemporized a thatch for the roofless cabin, and the Duchess directed Piney in the rearrangement of the interior with a taste and tact that opened the blue eyes of that provincial maiden to their fullest extent. "I reckon now you're used to fine things at Poker Flat," said Piney. The Duchess turned away sharply to conceal something that reddened her cheeks through their professional tint, and Mother Shipton requested Piney not to "chatter."

But when Mr. Oakhurst returned from a weary search for the trail, he heard the sound of happy laughter echoed from the rocks. He stopped in some alarm, and his thoughts first naturally reverted to the whiskey, which he had prudently cached. "And yet it don't somehow sound like whiskey," said the gambler. It was not until he caught sight of the blazing fire through the still blinding storm, and the group around it, that he settled to the conviction that it was "square fun."

Whether Mr. Oakhurst had cached his cards with the whiskey as something debarred the free access of the community, I cannot say. It was certain that, in Mother Shipton's words, he "didn't say 'cards' once" during that evening. Haply the time was beguiled by an accordion, produced somewhat ostentatiously by Tom Simson from his pack. Notwithstanding some difficulties attending the manipulation of this instrument, Piney Woods managed to pluck several reluctant melodies from its keys to an accompaniment by the Innocent on a pair of bone castanets. But the crowning festivity of the evening was reached in a rude camp-meeting hymn, which the lovers, joining hands, sang with great earnestness and vociferation. I fear that a certain defiant tone and covenanter's swing to its chorus, rather than any devotional quality, caused it speedily to infect the others, who at last joined in the refrain:

"I'm proud to live in the service of the Lord,
    And I'm bound to die in His army."

The pines rocked, the storm eddied and whirled above the miserable group, and the flames of their altar leaped heavenward, as if in token of the vow.

At midnight the storm abated, the rolling clouds parted, and the stars glittered keenly above the sleeping camp. Mr. Oakhurst, whose professional habits had enabled him to live on the smallest possible amount of sleep, in dividing the watch with Tom Simson somehow managed to take upon himself the greater part of that duty. He excused himself to the Innocent by saying that he had "often been a week without sleep." "Doing what?" asked Tom. "Poker!" replied Oakhurst sententiously. "When a man gets a streak of luck—nigger-luck—he don't get tired. The luck gives in first. Luck," continued the gambler reflectively, "is a mighty queer thing. All you know about it for certain is that it's bound to change. And it's finding out when it's going to change that makes you. We've had a streak of bad luck since we left Poker Flat—you come along, and slap you get into it, too. If you can hold your cards right along you're all right. For," added the gambler, with cheerful irrelevance—

> " 'I'm proud to live in the service of the Lord,
> And I'm bound to die in His army.' "

The third day came, and the sun, looking through the white-curtained valley, saw the outcasts divide their slowly decreasing store of provision for the morning meal. It was one of the peculiarities of that mountain climate that its rays diffused a kindly warmth over the wintry landscape, as if in regretful commiseration of the past. But it revealed drift on drift of snow piled high around the hut—a hopeless, uncharted, trackless sea of white lying below the rocky shores to which the castaways still clung. Through the marvelously clear air the smoke of the pastoral village of Poker Flat rose miles away. Mother Shipton saw it, and from a remote pinnacle of her rocky fastness hurled in that direction a final malediction. It was her last vituperative attempt, and perhaps for that reason was invested with a certain degree of sublimity. It did her good, she privately informed the Duchess. "Just you go out there and cuss, and see." She then set herself to the task of amusing "the child," as she and the Duchess were pleased to call Piney. Piney was no chicken, but it was a soothing and original theory of the pair thus to account for the fact that she didn't swear and wasn't improper.

When night crept up again through the gorges, the reedy notes of the accordion rose and fell in fitful spasms and long-drawn gasps by the flickering camp-fire. But music failed to fill entirely the aching void left by insufficient food, and a new diversion was proposed by Piney—storytelling. Neither Mr. Oakhurst nor his female companions caring to relate their personal experiences, this plan would have failed too, but for the Innocent. Some months before he had chanced upon a stray copy of Mr. Pope's ingenious translation of the Iliad. He now proposed to narrate the principal incidents of that poem—having thoroughly mastered the argument and fairly forgotten the words—in the current vernacular of Sandy Bar. And so for the rest of that night the Homeric demigods again walked the earth. Trojan bully and wily Greek wrestled in the winds, and the great pines in the canyon seemed to bow to the wrath of the son of Peleus. Mr. Oakhurst listened with quiet satisfaction. Most especially was he interested in the fate of "Ash-heels," as the Innocent persisted in denominating the "swift-footed Achilles."

So, with small food and much of Homer and the accordion, a week passed over the heads of the outcasts. The sun again forsook them, and again from leaden skies the snowflakes were sifted over the land. Day by day closer around them drew the snowy circle, until at last they looked from their prison over drifted walls of dazzling white that towered twenty feet above their heads. It became more and more difficult to replenish their fires, even from the fallen trees beside them, now half hidden in the drifts. And yet no one complained. The lovers turned from the dreary prospect and looked into each other's eyes, and were happy. Mr. Oakhurst settled himself coolly to the losing game before him. The Duchess, more cheerful than she had been, assumed the care of Piney. Only Mother Shipton—once the strongest of the party—seemed to sicken and fade. At midnight on the tenth day she called Oakhurst to her side. "I'm going," she said, in a voice of querulous weakness, "but don't say anything about it. Don't waken the kids. Take the bundle from under my head, and open it." Mr. Oakhurst did so. It contained Mother Shipton's rations for the last week, untouched. "Give 'em to the child," she said, pointing to the sleeping Piney. "You've starved yourself," said the gambler. "That's what they call it," said the woman querulously, as she lay down again, and turning her face to the wall, passed quietly away.

The accordion and the bones were put aside that day, and Homer was forgotten. When the body of Mother Shipton had been committed to the snow, Mr. Oakhurst took the Innocent aside, and showed him a pair of snowshoes, which he had fashioned from the old pack-saddle. "There's one chance in a hundred to save her yet," he said, pointing to Piney; "but it's there," he added, pointing toward Poker Flat. "If you can reach there in two days she's safe." "And you?" asked Tom Simson. "I'll stay here," was the curt reply.

The lovers parted with a long embrace. "You are not going, too?" said the Duchess, as she saw Mr. Oakhurst apparently waiting to accompany him. "As far as the canyon," he replied. He turned suddenly and kissed the Duchess, leaving her pallid face aflame, and her trembling limbs rigid with amazement.

Night came, but not Mr. Oakhurst. It brought the storm again and the whirling snow. Then the Duchess, feeding the fire, found that someone had quietly piled beside the hut enough fuel to last a few days longer. The tears rose to her eyes, but she hid them from Piney.

The women slept but little. In the morning, looking into each other's faces, they read their fate. Neither spoke, but Piney, accepting the position of the stronger, drew near and placed her arm around the Duchess's waist. They kept this attitude for the rest of the day. That night the storm reached its greatest fury, and rending asunder the protecting vines, invaded the very hut.

Toward morning they found themselves unable to feed the fire, which gradually died away. As the embers slowly blackened, the Duchess crept closer to Piney, and broke the silence of many hours: "Piney, can you pray?" "No, dear," said Piney simply. The Duchess, without knowing exactly why, felt relieved, and putting her head upon Piney's shoulder, spoke no more. And so reclining, the younger and purer pillowing the head of her soiled sister upon her virgin breast, they fell asleep.

The wind lulled as if it feared to waken them. Feathery drifts of snow, shaken from the long pine boughs, flew like white winged birds, and settled about them as they slept. The moon through the rifted clouds looked down upon what had been the camp. But all human stain, all trace of earthly travail, was hidden beneath the spotless mantle mercifully flung from above.

They slept all that day and the next, nor did they waken when voices and footsteps broke the silence of the camp. And when pitying fingers brushed the snow from their wan faces, you could scarcely have told from the equal peace that dwelt upon them which was she that had sinned. Even the law of Poker Flat recognized this, and turned away, leaving them still locked in each other's arms.

But at the head of the gulch, on one of the largest pine trees, they found the deuce of clubs pinned to the bark with a bowie knife. It bore the following, written in pencil in a firm hand:

†

BENEATH THIS TREE

LIES THE BODY

OF

JOHN OAKHURST,

WHO STRUCK A STREAK OF BAD LUCK

ON THE 23D OF NOVEMBER, 1850,

AND

HANDED IN HIS CHECKS

ON THE 7TH DECEMBER, 1850.

↓

And pulseless and cold, with a derringer by his side and a bullet in his heart, though still calm as in life, beneath the snow lay he who was at once the strongest and yet the weakest of the outcasts of Poker Flat.

THE LUCK OF ROARING CAMP

There was commotion in Roaring Camp. It could not have been a fight, for in 1850 that was not novel enough to have called together the entire settlement. The ditches and claims were not only deserted, but "Tuttle's grocery" had contributed its gamblers, who, it will be remembered, calmly continued their game the day that French Pete and Kanaka Joe shot each other to death over the bar in the front room. The whole camp was collected before a rude cabin on the outer edge of the clearing. Conversation was carried on in a low tone, but the name of a woman was frequently repeated. It was a name familiar enough in the camp—"Cherokee Sal."

Perhaps the less said of her the better. She was a coarse and, it is to be feared, a very sinful woman. But at that time she was the only woman in Roaring Camp, and was just then lying in sore extremity, when she most needed the ministration of her own sex. Dissolute, abandoned, and irreclaimable, she was yet suffering a martyrdom hard enough to bear even when veiled by sympathizing womanhood, but now terrible in her loneliness. The primal curse had come to her in that

22

original isolation which must have made the punishment of the first transgression so dreadful. It was, perhaps, part of the expiation of her sin that, at a moment when she most lacked her sex's intuitive tenderness and care, she met only the half-contemptuous faces of her masculine associates. Yet a few of the spectators were, I think, touched by her sufferings. Sandy Tipton thought it was "rough on Sal," and in the contemplation of her condition, for a moment rose superior to the fact that he had an ace and two bowers in his sleeve.

It will be seen also that the situation was novel. Deaths were by no means uncommon in Roaring Camp, but a birth was a new thing. People had been dismissed from the camp effectively, finally, and with no possibility of return; but this was the first time that anybody had been introduced *ab initio*. Hence the excitement.

"You go in there, Stumpy," said a prominent citizen known as "Kentuck," addressing one of the loungers. "Go in there, and see what you kin do. You've had experience in them things."

Perhaps there was a fitness in the selection. Stumpy, in other climes, had been the putative head of two families; in fact, it was owing to some legal informality in these proceedings that Roaring Camp—a city of refuge—was indebted to his company. The crowd approved the choice, and Stumpy was wise enough to bow to the majority. The door closed on the extempore surgeon and midwife, and Roaring Camp sat down outside, smoked its pipe, and awaited the issue.

The assemblage numbered about a hundred men. One or two of these were actual fugitives from justice, some were criminal, and all were reckless. Physically they exhibited no indication of their past lives and character. The greatest scamp had a Raphael face, with a profusion of blond hair; Oakhurst, a gambler, had the melancholy air and intellectual abstraction of a Hamlet; the coolest and most courageous man was scarcely over five feet in height, with a soft voice and an embarrassed, timid manner. The term "roughs" applied to them was a distinction rather than a definition. Perhaps in the minor details of fingers, toes, ears, etc., the camp may have been deficient, but these slight omissions did not detract from their aggregate force. The strongest man had but three fingers on his right hand; the best shot had but one eye.

Such was the physical aspect of the men that were dispersed around the cabin. The camp lay in a triangular valley between two hills and a river. The only outlet was a steep trail over the summit of a hill that faced the cabin, now illuminated by the rising moon. The suffering woman might have seen it from the rude bunk whereon she lay—seen it winding like a silver thread until it was lost in the stars above.

A fire of withered pine boughs added sociability to the gathering. By degrees the natural levity of Roaring Camp returned. Bets were freely offered and taken regarding the results. Three to five that "Sal would get through with it"; even that the child would survive; side bets as to the sex and complexion of the coming stranger. In the midst of an excited discussion an exclamation came from those nearest the door, and the camp stopped to listen. Above the swaying and moaning of the pines, the swift rush of the river, and the crackling of the fire rose a sharp, querulous cry—a

cry unlike anything heard before in the camp. The
pines stopped moaning, the river ceased to rush, and
the fire to crackle. It seemed as if Nature had stopped
to listen too.

·The camp rose to its feet as one man! It was proposed to explode a barrel of gunpowder; but in consideration of the situation of the mother, better counsels
prevailed, and only a few revolvers were discharged;
for whether owing to the rude surgery of the camp,
or some other reason, Cherokee Sal was sinking fast.
Within an hour she had climbed, as it were, that rug-·
ged road that led to the stars, and so passed out of
Roaring Camp, its sin and shame, forever. I do not
think that the announcement disturbed them much,
except in speculation as to the fate of the child. "Can
he live now?" was asked of Stumpy. The answer was
doubtful. The only other being of Cherokee Sal's sex
and maternal condition in the settlement was an ass.
There was some conjecture as to fitness, but the ex-
periment was tried. It was less problematical than the
ancient treatment of Romulus and Remus, and apparently as successful.

When these details were completed, which exhausted another hour, the door was opened, and the
anxious crowd of men, who had already formed themselves into a queue, entered in single file. Beside the
low bunk or shelf, on which the figure of the mother
was starkly outlined below the blankets, stood a pine
table. On this a candlebox was placed, and within it,
swathed in staring red flannel, lay the last arrival at
Roaring Camp. Beside the candlebox was placed a
hat. Its use was soon indicated "Gentlemen," and
Stumpy, with a singular mixture of authority and *ex*

officio complacency—"gentlemen will please pass in at the front door, round the table, and out at the back door. Them as wishes to contribute anything toward the orphan will find a hat handy." The first man entered with his hat on; he uncovered, however, as he looked about him, and so unconsciously set an example to the next. In such communities good and bad actions are catching. As the procession filed in comments were audible—criticisms addressed perhaps rather to Stumpy in the character of showman: "Is that him?" "Mighty small specimen"; "Hasn't more'n got the color"; "Ain't bigger nor a derringer." The contributions were as characteristic: A silver tobacco box; a doubloon; a navy revolver, silver mounted; a gold specimen; a very beautifully embroidered lady's handkerchief (from Oakhurst the gambler); a diamond breastpin; a diamond ring (suggested by the pin, with the remark from the giver that he "saw that pin and went two diamonds better"); a slung shot; a Bible (contributor not detected); a golden spur; a silver teaspoon (the initials, I regret to say, were not the giver's); a pair of surgeon's shears; a lancet; a Bank of England note for £5; and about $200 in loose gold and silver coin. During these proceedings Stumpy maintained a silence as impassive as the dead on his left, a gravity as inscrutable as that of the newly born on his right. Only one incident occurred to break the monotony of the curious procession. As Kentuck bent over the candlebox half curiously, the child turned, and, in a spasm of pain, caught at his groping finger and held it fast for a moment. Kentuck looked foolish and embarrassed. Something like a blush tried to assert itself in his weather-beaten cheek. "The d—d little cuss!" he said, as he extricated his finger, with perhaps more tenderness and care than he might have been deemed capable of showing. He held that finger a little apart from its fellows as he went out, and examined it curiously. The examination provoked the same original remark in regard to the child. In fact, he seemed to enjoy repeating it. "He rastled with my finger," he remarked to Tipton, holding up the member, "the d——d little cuss!"

It was four o'clock before the camp sought repose. A light burnt in the cabin where the watchers sat, for Stumpy did not go to bed that night. Nor did Kentuck. He drank quite freely, and related with great gusto his experience, invariably ending with his characteristic condemnation of the newcomer. It seemed to relieve him of any unjust implication of sentiment, and Kentuck had the weaknesses of the nobler sex. When everybody else had gone to bed, he walked down to the river and whistled reflectingly. Then he walked up the gulch past the cabin, still whistling with demonstrative unconcern. At a large redwood tree he paused and retraced his steps, and again passed the cabin. Halfway down to the river's bank he again paused, and then returned and knocked at the door. It was opened by Stumpy. "How goes it?" said Kentuck, looking past Stumpy toward the candlebox. "All serene!" replied Stumpy. "Anything up?" "Nothing." There was a pause—an embarrassing one—Stumpy still holding the door. Then Kentuck had recourse to his finger, which he held up to Stumpy. "Rastled with it—the d——d little cuss," he said, and retired.

The next day Cherokee Sal had such rude sepulture as Roaring Camp afforded. After her body had been committed to the hillside, there was a formal meeting of the camp to discuss what should be done with her infant. A resolution to adopt it was unanimous and enthusiastic. But an animated discussion in regard to the manner and feasibility of providing for its wants at once sprang up. It was remarkable that the argument partook of none of those fierce personalities with which discussions were usually conducted at Roaring Camp. Tipton proposed that they should send the child to Red Dog—a distance of forty miles —where female attention could be procured. But the unlucky suggestion met with fierce and unanimous opposition. It was evident that no plan which entailed parting from their new acquisition would for a moment be entertained. "Besides," said Tom Ryder, "them fellows at Red Dog would swap it, and ring in somebody else on us." A disbelief in the honesty of other camps prevailed at Roaring Camp, as in other places.

The introduction of a female nurse in the camp also met with objection. It was argued that no decent woman could be prevailed to accept Roaring Camp as her home, and the speaker urged that "they didn't want any more of the other kind." This unkind allusion to the defunct mother, harsh as it may seem, was the first spasm of propriety—the first symptom of the camp's regeneration. Stumpy advanced nothing. Perhaps he felt a certain delicacy in interfering with the selection of a possible successor in office. But when questioned, he averred stoutly that he and "Jinny" —the mammal before alluded to—could manage to rear the child. There was something original, independent, and heroic about the plan that pleased the camp. Stumpy was retained. Certain articles were sent for to Sacramento. "Mind," said the treasurer, as he pressed a bag of gold dust into the expressman's hand, "the best that can be got—lace, you know, and filigree work and frills—d—n the cost!"

Strange to say, the child thrived. Perhaps the invigorating climate of the mountain camp was compensation for material deficiencies. Nature took the foundling to her broader breast. In that rare atmosphere of the Sierra foothills—that air pungent with balsamic odor, that ethereal cordial at once bracing and exhilarating—he may have found food and nourishment, or a subtle chemistry that transmuted ass's milk to lime and phosphorus. Stumpy inclined to the belief that it was the latter and good nursing. "Me and that ass," he would say, "has been father and mother to him! Don't you," he would add, apostrophizing the helpless bundle before him, "never to go back on us."

By the time he was a month old the necessity of giving him a name became apparent. He had generally been known as "the Kid," "Stumpy's Boy," "The Coyote" (an allusion to his vocal powers), and even by Kentuck's endearing diminutive of "The d—d little cuss." But these were felt to be vague and unsatisfactory, and were at last dismissed under another influence. Gamblers and adventurers are generally superstitious, and Oakhurst one day declared that the baby had brought "the luck" to Roaring Camp. It was certain that of late they had been successful. "Luck" was the name agreed upon, with the prefix of Tommy for greater convenience. No allusion was made to the mother, and the father was unknown. "It's better," said the philosophical Oakhurst, "to take a fresh deal all round. Call him Luck, and start him fair." A day was accordingly set apart for the christening. What was meant by this ceremony the reader may imagine who has already gathered some idea of the reckless irreverence of Roaring Camp. The master of ceremonies was one "Boston," a noted wag, and the occasion seemed to promise the greatest facetiousness. This ingenious satirist had spent two days in preparing a burlesque of the Church service, with pointed local allusions. The choir was properly trained, and Sandy Tipton was to stand godfather. But after the procession had marched to the grove with music and banners, and the child had been deposited before a mock altar, Stumpy stepped before the expectant crowd. "It ain't my style to spoil fun, boys," said the little man, stoutly eying the faces around him, "but it strikes me that this thing ain't exactly on the squar. It's playing it pretty low down on this yer baby to ring in fun on him that he ain't goin' to understand. And ef there's goin' to be any godfathers round, I'd like to see who's got any better rights than me." A silence followed Stumpy's speech. To the credit of all humorists be it said that the first man to acknowledge its justice was the satirist thus stopped of his fun. "But," said Stumpy, quickly following up his advantage, "we're here for a christening, and we'll have it. I proclaim you Thomas Luck, according to the laws of the United States and the State of California, so help me God." It was the first time that the name of the Deity had been otherwise uttered than profanely in the camp. The form of christening was perhaps even more ludicrous than the satirist had conceived; but strangely enough, nobody saw it and nobody laughed. "Tommy" was christened as seriously as he would have been under a Christian roof, and cried and was comforted in as orthodox fashion.

And so the work of regeneration began in Roaring Camp. Almost imperceptibly a change came over the settlement. The cabin assigned to "Tommy Luck"— or "The Luck," as he was more frequently called— first showed signs of improvement. It was kept scrupulously clean and whitewashed. Then it was boarded, clothed, and papered. The rosewood cradle, packed eighty miles by mule, had, in Stumpy's way of putting it, "sorter killed the rest of the furniture." So the rehabilitation of the camp became a necessity. The men who were in the habit of lounging in at Stumpy's to see "how 'The Luck' got on" seemed to appreciate the change, and in self-defense the rival establishment of "Tuttle's grocery" bestirred itself and imported a carpet and mirrors. The reflections of the latter on the appearance of Roaring Camp tended to produce stricter habits of personal cleanliness. Again Stumpy imposed a kind of quarantine upon those who aspired to the honor and privilege of holding The Luck. It was a cruel mortification to Kentuck—who, in the carelessness of a large nature and the habits of frontier life, had begun to regard all garments as a second cuticle, which, like a snake's, only sloughed off through decay—to be debarred this privilege from certain prudential reasons. Yet such was the subtle influence of innovation that he thereafter appeared regularly every afternoon in a clean shirt and face still shining from his ablutions. Nor were moral and social sanitary laws neglected. "Tommy," who was supposed to

spend his whole existence in a persistent attempt to
repose, must not be disturbed by noise. The shouting
and yelling, which had gained the camp its infelicitous
title, were not permitted within hearing distance of
Stumpy's. The men conversed in whispers or smoked
with Indian gravity. Profanity was tacitly given up in
these sacred precincts, and throughout the camp a
popular form of expletive, known as "D—n the luck!"
and "Curse the luck!" was abandoned, as having a
new personal bearing. Vocal music was not inter-
dicted, being supposed to have a soothing, tranquil-
izing quality; and one song, sung by "Man-o'-War
Jack," an English sailor from her Majesty's Austral-
ian colonies, was quite popular as a lullaby. It was a
lugubrious recital of the exploits of "the Arethusa,
Seventy-four," in a muffled minor, ending with a prolonged dying fall at the burden of each verse, "On
b-oo-o-ard of the Arethusa." It was a fine sight to see
Jack holding The Luck, rocking from side to side as
if with the motion of a ship, and crooning forth this
naval ditty. Either through the peculiar rocking of
Jack or the length of his song—it contained ninety
stanzas, and was continued with conscientious deliberation to the bitter end—the lullaby generally had
the desired effect. At such times the men would lie at
full length under the trees in the soft summer twilight,
smoking their pipes and drinking in the melodious utterances. An indistinct idea that this was pastoral happiness pervaded the camp. "This 'ere kind o' think,"
said the Cockney Simmons, meditatively reclining
on his elbow, "is 'evingly." It reminded him of
Greenwich.

On the long summer days The Luck was usually

carried to the gulch from whence the golden store of
Roaring Camp was taken. There, on a blanket spread
over pine boughs, he would lie while the men were
working in the ditches below. Latterly there was a
rude attempt to decorate this bower with flowers and
sweet-smelling shrubs, and generally some one would
bring him a cluster of wild honeysuckles, azaleas, or
the painted blossoms of Las Mariposas. The men had
suddenly awakened to the fact that there were beauty
and significance in these trifles, which they had so
long trodden carelessly beneath their feet. A flake of
glittering mica, a fragment of variegated quartz, a
bright pebble from the bed of the creek, became beautiful to eyes thus cleared and strengthened, and were
invariably put aside for The Luck. It was wonderful
how many treasures the woods and hillsides yielded
that "would do for Tommy." Surrounded by play-
things such as never child out of fairyland had before, it is to be hoped that Tommy was content. He
appeared to be serenely happy, albeit there was an in-
fantine gravity about him, a contemplative light in
his round gray eyes, that sometimes worried Stumpy.
He was always tractable and quiet, and it is recorded
that once, having crept beyond his "corral"—a hedge
of tessellated pine boughs, which surrounded his bed
—he dropped over the bank on his head in the soft
earth, and remained with his mottled legs in the air
in that position for at least five minutes with unflinch-
ing gravity. He was extricated without a murmur. I
hesitate to record the many other instances of his sa-
gacity, which rest, unfortunately, upon the statements
of prejudiced friends. Some of them were not without a tinge of superstition. "I crep' up the bank just

now," said Kentuck one day, in a breathless state of excitement, "and dern my skin if he wasn't a-talking to a jay bird as was a-sittin' on his lap. There they was, just as free and sociable as anything you please, a-jawin' at each other just like two cherrybums." Howbeit, whether creeping over the pine boughs or lying lazily on his back blinking at the leaves above him, to him the birds sang, the squirrels chattered, and the flowers bloomed. Nature was his nurse and play-fellow. For him she would let slip between the leaves golden shafts of sunlight that fell just within his grasp; she would send wandering breezes to visit him with the balm of bay and resinous gum; to him the tall red-woods nodded familiarly and sleepily, the bumblebees buzzed, and the rooks cawed a slumbrous accompaniment.

Such was the golden summer of Roaring Camp. They were "flush times," and the luck was with them. The claims had yielded enormously. The camp was jealous of its privileges and looked suspiciously on strangers. No encouragement was given to immigra-tion, and, to make their seclusion more perfect, the land on either side of the mountain wall that sur-rounded the camp they duly preempted. This, and a reputation for singular proficiency with the revolver, kept the reserve of Roaring Camp inviolate. The ex-pressman—their only connecting link with the sur-rounding world—sometimes told wonderful stories of the camp. He would say, "They've a street up there in 'Roaring' that would lay over any street in Red Dog. They've got vines and flowers round their houses, and they wash themselves twice a day. But they're

mighty rough on strangers, and they worship an In-
gin baby."

With the prosperity of the camp came a desire for
further improvement. It was proposed to build a hotel
in the following spring, and to invite one or two decent
families to reside there for the sake of The Luck, who
might perhaps profit by female companionship. The
sacrifice that this concession to the sex cost these men,
who were fiercely skeptical in regard to its general vir-
tue and usefulness, can only be accounted for by
their affection for Tommy. A few still held out. But
the resolve could not be carried into effect for three
months, and the minority meekly yielded in the hope
that something might turn up to prevent it. And it
did.

The winter of 1851 will long be remembered in the
foothills. The snow lay deep on the Sierras, and every mountain creek became a river, and every river a
lake. Each gorge and gulch was transformed into a
tumultuous watercourse that descended the hillsides,
tearing down giant trees and scattering its drift and
debris along the plain. Red Dog had been twice under
water, and Roaring Camp had been forewarned: "Water put the gold into them gulches," said Stumpy. "It's
been here once and will be here again!" And that
night the North Fork suddenly leaped over its banks
and swept up the triangular valley of Roaring Camp.

In the confusion of rushing water, crashing trees,
and crackling timber, and the darkness which seemed
to flow with the water and blot out the fair valley, but
little could be done to collect the scattered camp.
When the morning broke, the cabin of Stumpy, near-

est the river-bank, was gone. Higher up the gulch they found the body of its unlucky owner; but the pride, the hope, the joy, The Luck, of Roaring Camp had disappeared. They were returning with sad hearts when a shout from the bank recalled them.

It was a relief-boat from down the river. They had picked up, they said, a man and an infant, nearly exhausted, about two miles below. Did anybody know them, and did they belong here?

It needed but a glance to show them Kentuck lying there, cruelly crushed and bruised, but still holding The Luck of Roaring Camp in his arms. As they bent over the strangely assorted pair, they saw that the child was cold and pulseless. "He is dead," said one. Kentuck opened his eyes. "Dead?" he repeated feebly. "Yes, my man, and you are dying too." A smile lit the eyes of the expiring Kentuck. "Dying!" he repeated; "he's a-taking me with him. Tell the boys I've got The Luck with me now"; and the strong man, clinging to the frail babe as a drowning man is said to cling to a straw, drifted away into the shadowy river that flows forever to the unknown sea.

TENNESSEE'S PARTNER

I do not think that we ever knew his real name. Our ignorance of it certainly never gave us any social inconvenience, for at Sandy Bar in 1854 most men were christened anew. Sometimes these appellatives were derived from some distinctiveness of dress, as in the case of "Dungaree Jack"; or from some peculiarity of habit, as shown in "Saleratus Bill," so called from an undue proportion of that chemical in his daily bread; or from some unlucky slip, as exhibited in "The Iron Pirate," a mild, inoffensive man, who earned that baleful title by his unfortunate mispronunciation of the term "iron pyrites." Perhaps this may have been the beginning of a rude heraldry; but I am constrained to think that it was because a man's real name in that day rested solely upon his own unsupported statement. "Call yourself Clifford, do you?" said Boston, addressing a timid newcomer with infinite scorn; "Hell is full of such Cliffords!" He then introduced the unfortunate man, whose name happened to be really Clifford, as "Jaybird Charley,"—an unhallowed inspiration of the moment that clung to him ever after.

37

But to return to Tennessee's Partner, whom we never knew by any other than this relative title. That he had ever existed as a separate and distinct individuality we only learned later. It seems that in 1853 he left Poker Flat to go to San Francisco, ostensibly to procure a wife. He never got any farther than Stockton. At that place he was attracted by a young person who waited upon the table at the hotel where he took his meals. One morning he said something to her which caused her to smile not unkindly, to somewhat coquettishly break a plate of toast over his upturned, serious, simple face, and to retreat to the kitchen. He followed her, and emerged a few moments later, covered with more toast and victory. That day week they were married by a justice of the peace, and returned to Poker Flat. I am aware that something more might be made of this episode, but I prefer to tell it as it was current at Sandy Bar—in the gulches and barrooms—where all sentiment was modified by a strong sense of humor.

Of their married felicity but little is known, perhaps for the reason that Tennessee, then living with his partner, one day took occasion to say something to the bride on his own account, at which, it is said, she smiled not unkindly and chastely retreated—this time as far as Marysville, where Tennessee followed her, and where they went to housekeeping without the aid of a justice of the peace. Tennessee's Partner took the loss of his wife simply and seriously, as was his fashion. But to everybody's surprise, when Tennessee one day returned from Marysville, without his partner's wife—she having smiled and retreated with somebody else—Tennessee's Partner was the first man to shake his hand and greet him with affection. The boys who had gathered in the canyon to see the shooting were naturally indignant. Their indignation might have found vent in sarcasm but for a certain look in Tennessee's Partner's eye that indicated a lack of humorous appreciation. In fact, he was a grave man, with a steady application to practical detail which was unpleasant in a difficulty.

Meanwhile a popular feeling against Tennessee had grown up on the Bar. He was known to be a gambler; he was suspected to be a thief. In these suspicions Tennessee's Partner was equally compromised; his continued intimacy with Tennessee after the affair above quoted could only be accounted for on the hypothesis of a copartnership of crime. At last Tennessee's guilt became flagrant. One day he overtook a stranger on his way to Red Dog. The stranger afterward related that Tennessee beguiled the time with interesting anecdote and reminiscence, but illogically concluded the interview in the following words: "And now, young man, I'll trouble you for your knife, your pistols, and your money. You see your weppings might get you into trouble at Red Dog, and your money's temptation to the evilly disposed. I think you said your address was San Francisco. I shall endeavor to call." It may be stated here that Tennessee had a fine flow of humor, which no business preoccupation could wholly subdue.

This exploit was his last. Red Dog and Sandy Bar made common cause against the highwayman. Tennessee was hunted in very much the same fashion as his prototype, the grizzly. As the toils closed around him, he made a desperate dash through the Bar, emptying his revolver at the crowd before the Arcade Saloon, and so on up Grizzly Canyon; but at its farther extremity he was stopped by a small man on a gray horse. The men looked at each other a moment in silence. Both were fearless, both self-possessed and independent, and both types of a civilization that in the seventeenth century would have been called heroic, but in the nineteenth simply "reckless."

"What have you got there?—I call," said Tennessee quietly.

"Two bowers and an ace," said the stranger as quietly, showing two revolvers and a bowie knife.

"That takes me," returned Tennessee; and with this gambler's epigram, he threw away his useless pistol and rode back with his captor.

It was a warm night. The cool breeze which usually sprang up with the going down of the sun behind the chaparral-crested mountain was that evening withheld from Sandy Bar. The little canyon was stifling with heated resinous odors, and the decaying driftwood on the Bar sent forth faint sickening exhalations. The feverishness of day and its fierce passions still filled the camp. Lights moved restlessly along the bank of the river, striking no answering reflection from its tawny current. Against the blackness of the pines the windows of the old loft above the express office stood out staringly bright; and through their curtainless panes the loungers below could see the forms of those who were even then deciding the fate of Tennessee. And above all this, etched on the dark firmament, rose the Sierra, remote and passionless, crowned with remoter passionless stars.

The trial of Tennessee was conducted as fairly as

was consistent with a judge and jury who felt themselves to some extent obliged to justify, in their verdict, the previous irregularities of arrest and indict-
ment. The law of Sandy Bar was implacable, but not
vengeful. The excitement and personal feeling of the
chase were over; with Tennessee safe in their hands,
they were ready to listen patiently to any defense,
which they were already satisfied was insufficient.
There being no doubt in their own minds, they were
willing to give the prisoner the benefit of any that
might exist. Secure in the hypothesis that he ought to
be hanged on general principles, they indulged him
with more latitude of defense than his reckless hardihood seemed to ask. The Judge appeared to be more
anxious than the prisoner, who, otherwise uncon-
cerned, evidently took a grim pleasure in the responsibility he had created. "I don't take any hand in this
yer game," had been his invariable but good-humored
reply to all questions. The Judge—who was also his
captor—for a moment vaguely regretted that he had
not shot him "on sight" that morning, but presently
dismissed this human weakness as unworthy of the
judicial mind. Nevertheless, when there was a tap at
the door, and it was said that Tennessee's Partner was
there on behalf of the prisoner, he was admitted at
once without question. Perhaps the younger members
of the jury, to whom the proceedings were becoming
irksomely thoughtful, hailed him as a relief.

For he was not, certainly, an imposing figure. Short
and stout, with a square face, sunburned into a pre-
ternatural redness, clad in a loose duck "jumper"
and trousers streaked and splashed with red soil, his
aspect under any circumstances would have been

quaint, and was now even ridiculous. As he stooped to deposit at his feet a heavy carpetbag he was carrying, it became obvious, from partially developed legends and inscriptions, that the material with which his trousers had been patched had been originally intended for a less ambitious covering. Yet he advanced with great gravity, and after shaking the hand of each person in the room with labored cordiality, he wiped his serious perplexed face on a red bandana handkerchief, a shade lighter than his complexion, laid his powerful hand upon the table to steady himself, and thus addressed the Judge:

"I was passin' by," he began, by way of apology, "and I thought I'd just step in and see how things was gittin' on with Tennessee thar—my pardner. It's a hot night. I disremember any sich weather before on the Bar."

He paused a moment, but nobody volunteering any other meteorological recollection, he again had recourse to his pocket handkerchief, and for some moments mopped his face diligently.

"Have you anything to say on behalf of the prisoner?" said the Judge finally.

"Thet's it," said Tennessee's Partner, in a tone of relief. "I come yar as Tennessee's pardner—knowing him nigh on four year, off and on, wet and dry, in luck and out o' luck. His ways ain't aller my ways, but thar ain't any p'ints in that young man, thar ain't any liveliness as he's been up to, as I don't know. And you sez to me, sez you—confidential-like, and between man and man—sez you, 'Do you know anything in his behalf?' and I sez to you, sez I—confidential-like, as between man and man—'What should a man know of his pardner?' "

"Is this all you have to say?" asked the Judge impatiently, feeling, perhaps, that a dangerous sympathy of humor was beginning to humanize the court.

"Thet's so," continued Tennessee's Partner. "It ain't for me to say anything agin' him. And now, what's the case? Here's Tennessee wants money, wants it bad, and doesn't like to ask it of his old pardner. Well, what does Tennessee do? He lays for a stranger, and he fetches that stranger; and you lays for *him*, and you fetches *him;* and the honors is easy. And I put it to you, bein' a fa'r-minded man, and to you, gentlemen all, as fa'r-minded men, ef this isn't so."

"Prisoner," said the Judge, interrupting, "have you any questions to ask this man?"

"No! no!" continued Tennessee's Partner hastily. "I play this yer hand alone. To come down to the bedrock, it's just this: Tennessee thar has played it pretty rough and expensivelike on a stranger, and on this yer camp. And now, what's the fair thing? Some would say more, some would say less. Here's seventeen hundred dollars in coarse gold and a watch—it's about all my pile—and call it square!" And before a hand could be raised to prevent him, he had emptied the contents of the carpetbag upon the table.

For a moment his life was in jeopardy. One or two men sprang to their feet, several hands groped for hidden weapons, and a suggestion to "throw him from the window" was only overridden by a gesture from the Judge. Tennessee laughed. And apparently oblivious of the excitement, Tennessee's Partner improved the opportunity to mop his face again with his hand-kerchief.

When order was restored, and the man was made to understand by the use of forcible figures and rhetoric that Tennessee's offense could not be condoned by money, his face took a more serious and sanguinary hue, and those who were nearest to him noticed that his rough hand trembled slightly on the table. He hesitated a moment as he slowly returned the gold to the carpetbag, as if he had not yet entirely caught the elevated sense of justice which swayed the tribunal, and was perplexed with the belief that he had not offered enough. Then he turned to the Judge, and saying, "This yer is a lone hand, played alone, and without my pardner," he bowed to the jury and was about to withdraw, when the Judge called him back:

"If you have anything to say to Tennessee, you had better say it now."

For the first time that evening the eyes of the prisoner and his strange advocate met. Tennessee smiled, showed his white teeth, and saying, "Euchred, old man!" held out his hand. Tennessee's Partner took it in his own, and saying, "I just dropped in as I was passin' to see how things was gettin' on," let the hand passively fall, and adding that "it was a warm night," again mopped his face with his handkerchief, and without another word withdrew.

The two men never again met each other alive. For the unparalleled insult of a bribe offered to Judge Lynch—who, whether bigoted, weak, or narrow, was at least incorruptible—firmly fixed in the mind of that mythical personage any wavering determination of Tennessee's fate; and at the break of day he was marched, closely guarded, to meet it at the top of Marley's Hill.

How he met it, how cool he was, how he refused to say anything, how perfect were the arrangements of the committee, were all duly reported, with the addition of a warning moral and example to all future evil-doers, in the *Red Dog Clarion* by its editor, who was present, and to whose vigorous English I cheerfully refer the reader. But the beauty of that midsummer morning, the blessed amity of earth and air and sky, the awakened life of the free woods and hills, the joyous renewal and promise of Nature, and above all, the infinite serenity that thrilled through each, was not reported, as not being a part of the social lesson. And yet, when the weak and foolish deed was done, and a life, with its possibilities and responsibilities, had passed out of the misshapen thing that dangled between earth and sky, the birds sang, the flowers bloomed, the sun shone, as cheerily as before; and possibly the *Red Dog Clarion* was right.

Tennessee's Partner was not in the group that surrounded the ominous tree. But as they turned to disperse, attention was drawn to the sinular appearance of a motionless donkey cart halted at the side of the road. As they approached, they at once recognized the venerable Jenny and the two-wheeled cart as the property of Tennessee's Partner, used by him in carrying dirt from his claim; and a few paces distant the owner of the equipage himself, sitting under a buckeye tree, wiping the perspiration from his glowing face. In answer to an inquiry, he said he had come for the body of the "diseased," "if it was all the same to the committee." He didn't wish to "hurry anything"; he could "wait." He was not working that day; and when the gentlemen were done with the "diseased," he would take him. "Ef thar is any present," he added, in his simple, serious way, "as would care to jine in the fun'l, they kin come." Perhaps it was from a sense of humor, which I have already intimated was a feature of Sandy Bar—perhaps it was from something even better than that, but two thirds of the loungers accepted the invitation at once.

It was noon when the body of Tennessee was delivered into the hands of his partner. As the cart drew up to the fatal tree, we noticed that it contained a rough oblong box—apparently made from a section of sluicing—and half filled with bark and the tassels of pine. The cart was further decorated with slips of willow and made fragrant with buckeye blossoms. When the body was deposited in the box, Tennessee's Partner drew over it a piece of tarred canvas, and gravely mounting the narrow seat in front, with his feet upon the shafts, urged the little donkey forward. The equipage moved slowly on, at that decorous pace which was habitual with Jenny even under less solemn circumstances. The men—half curiously, half jestingly, but all good-humoredly—strolled along beside the cart, some in advance, some a little in the rear of the homely catafalque. But whether from the narrowing of the road or some present sense of decorum, as the cart passed on, the company fell to the rear in couples, keeping step, and otherwise assuming the external show of a formal procession. Jack Folinsbee, who had at the outset played a funeral march in dumb show upon an imaginary trombone, desisted from a lack of sympathy and appreciation—not having, perhaps, your true humorist's capacity to be content with the enjoyment of his own fun.

The way led through Grizzly Canyon, by this time clothed in funeral drapery and shadows. The red-woods, burying their moccasined feet in the red soil, stood in Indian file along the track, trailing an uncouth benediction from their bending boughs upon the passing bier. A hare, surprised into helpless inactivity, sat upright and pulsating in the ferns by the roadside as the cortege went by. Squirrels hastened to gain a secure outlook from higher boughs; and the blue jays, spreading their wings, fluttered before them like outriders, until the outskirts of Sandy Bar were reached, and the solitary cabin of Tennessee's Partner.

Viewed under more favorable circumstances, it would not have been a cheerful place. The unpicturesque site, the rude and unlovely outlines, the unsavory details, which distinguish the nest-building of the California miner, were all here with the dreariness of decay superadded. A few paces from the cabin there was a rough enclosure, which, in the brief days of Tennessee's Partner's matrimonial felicity, had been used as a garden, but was now overgrown with fern. As we approached it, we were surprised to find that what we had taken for a recent attempt at cultivation was the broken soil about an open grave.

The cart was halted before the enclosure, and rejecting the offers of assistance with the same air of simple self-reliance he had displayed throughout, Tennessee's Partner lifted the rough coffin on his back, and deposited it unaided within the shallow grave. He then nailed down the board which served as a lid, and mounting the little mound of earth beside it, took

off his hat and slowly mopped his face with his handkerchief. This the crowd felt was a preliminary
to speech, and they disposed themselves variously on
stumps and boulders, and sat expectant.

"When a man," began Tennessee's Partner slowly,
"has been running free all day, what's the natural
thing for him to do? Why, to come home. And if he
ain't in a condition to go home, what can his best
friend do? Why, bring him home. And here's Tennessee has been running free, and we brings him home
from his wandering." He paused and picked up a fragment of quartz, rubbed it thoughtfully on his sleeve,
and went on: "It ain't the first time that I've packed
him on my back, as you see'd me now. It ain't the first
time that I brought him to this yer cabin when
he couldn't help himself; it ain't the first time that I
and Jinny have waited for him on yon hill, and picked
him up and so fetched him home, when he couldn't
speak and didn't know me. And now that it's the last
time, why"—he paused and rubbed the quartz gently
on his sleeve—"you see it's sort of rough on his
pardener. And now, gentlemen," he added abruptly,
picking up his long-handled shovel, "the fun'l's over;
and my thanks, and Tennessee's thanks, to you for
your trouble."

Resisting any proffers of assistance, he began to fill
in the grave, turning his back upon the crowd, that
after a few moments' hesitation gradually withdrew.
As they crossed the little ridge that hid Sandy Bar
from view, some, looking back, thought they could see
Tennessee's Partner, his work done, sitting upon the
grave, his shovel between his knees, and his face
buried in his red bandana handkerchief. But it was

argued by others that you couldn't tell his face from his handkerchief at that distance, and this point remained undecided.

In the reaction that followed the feverish excitement of that day, Tennessee's Partner was not forgotten. A secret investigation had cleared him of any complicity in Tennessee's guilt, and left only a suspicion of his general sanity. Sandy Bar made a point of calling on him, and proffering various uncouth but well-meant kindnesses. But from that day his rude health and great strength seemed visibly to decline; and when the rainy season fairly set in, and the tiny grass blades were beginning to peep from the rocky mound above Tennessee's grave, he took to his bed.

One night, when the pines beside the cabin were swaying in the storm and trailing their slender fingers over the roof, and the roar and rush of the swollen river were heard below, Tennessee's Partner lifted his head from the pillow, saying, "It is time to go for Tennessee; I must put Jinny in the cart"; and would have risen from his bed but for the restraint of his attendant. Struggling, he still pursued his singular fancy: "There, now, steady, Jinny, steady, old girl. How dark it is! Look out for the ruts, and look out for him, too, old gal. Sometimes, you know, when he's blind drunk, he drops down right in the trail. Keep on straight up to the pine on the top of the hill. Thar! I told you so!—thar he is—coming this way, too—all by himself, sober, and his face a-shining. Tennessee! Pardner!"

And so they met.

THE IDYL OF
RED GULCH

Sandy was very drunk. He was lying under an azalea bush, in pretty much the same attitude in which he had fallen some hours before. How long he had been lying there he could not tell, and didn't care; how long he should lie there was a matter equally indefinite and unconsidered. A tranquil philosophy, born of his physical condition, suffused and saturated his moral being.

The spectacle of a drunken man, and of this drunken man in particular, was not, I grieve to say, of sufficient novelty in Red Gulch to attract attention. Earlier in the day some local satirist had erected a temporary tombstone at Sandy's head, bearing the inscription, "Effects of McCorkle's whiskey—kills at forty rods," with a hand pointing to McCorkle's saloon. But this, I imagine, was, like most local satire, personal; and was a reflection upon the unfairness of the process rather than a commentary upon the impropriety of the result. With this facetious exception, Sandy had been undisturbed. A wandering mule, released from his pack, had cropped the scant herbage beside him, and sniffed curiously at the prostrate man; a vagabond dog, with that deep sympathy which the species have for drunken men, had licked his dusty boots and curled himself up at his feet, and lay there, blinking one eye in the sunlight, with a simulation of dissipation that was ingenious and doglike in its implied flattery of the unconscious man beside him.

Meanwhile the shadows of the pine trees had slowly swung around until they crossed the road, and their trunks barred the open meadow with gigantic parallels of black and yellow. Little puffs of red dust, lifted by the plunging hoofs of passing teams, dispersed in a grimy shower upon the recumbent man. The sun sank lower and lower, and still Sandy stirred not. And then the repose of this philosopher was disturbed, as other philosophers have been, by the intrusion of an unphilosophical sex.

"Miss Mary," as she was known to the little flock that she had just dismissed from the log schoolhouse beyond the pines, was taking her afternoon walk. Observing an unusually fine cluster of blossoms on the azalea bush opposite, she crossed the road to pluck it, picking her way through the red dust, not without certain fierce little shivers of disgust and some feline circumlocution. And then she came suddenly upon Sandy!

Of course she uttered the little staccato cry of her sex. But when she had paid that tribute to her physical weakness she became overbold and halted for a moment—at least six feet from this prostrate monster—with her white skirts gathered in her hand, ready for flight. But neither sound nor motion came from the bush. With one little foot she then overturned the satirical headboard, and muttered "Beasts!"—

an epithet which probably, at that moment, conveniently classified in her mind the entire male population of Red Gulch. For Miss Mary, being possessed of certain rigid notions of her own, had not, perhaps, properly appreciated the demonstrative gallantry for which the Californian has been so justly celebrated by his brother Californians, and had, as a newcomer, perhaps fairly earned the reputation of being "stuck up."

As she stood there she noticed, also, that the slant sunbeams were heating Sandy's head to what she judged to be an unhealthy temperature, and that his hat was lying uselessly at his side. To pick it up and to place it over his face was a work requiring some courage, particularly as his eyes were open. Yet she did it and made good her retreat. But she was somewhat concerned, on looking back, to see that the hat was removed, and that Sandy was sitting up and saying something.

The truth was that in the calm depths of Sandy's mind he was satisfied that the rays of the sun were beneficial and healthful; that from childhood he had objected to lying down in a hat; that no people but condemned fools, past redemption, ever wore hats; and that his right to dispense with them when he pleased was inalienable. This was the statement of his inner consciousness. Unfortunately, its outward expression was vague, being limited to a repetition of the following formula: "Su'shine all ri'! Wasser maar, eh? Wass up, su'shine?"

Miss Mary stopped, and taking fresh courage from her vantage of distance, asked him if there was anything that he wanted.

"Wass up? Wasser maar?" continued Sandy, in a very high key.

"Get up, you horrid man!" said Miss Mary, now thoroughly incensed; "get up and go home."

Sandy staggered to his feet. He was six feet high, and Miss Mary trembled. He started forward a few paces and then stopped.

"Wass I go home for?" he suddenly asked, with great gravity.

"Go and take a bath," replied Miss Mary, eying his grimy person with great disfavor.

To her infinite dismay, Sandy suddenly pulled off his coat and vest, threw them on the ground, kicked off his boots, and plunging wildly forward, darted headlong over the hill in the direction of the river.

"Goodness heavens! the man will be drowned!" said Miss Mary; and then, with feminine inconsistency, she ran back to the schoolhouse and locked herself in.

That night, while seated at supper with her hostess, the blacksmith's wife, it came to Miss Mary to ask, demurely, if her husband ever got drunk. "Abner," responded Mrs. Stidger reflectively—"let's see! Abner hasn't been tight since last 'lection." Miss Mary would have liked to ask if he preferred lying in the sun on these occasions, and if a cold bath would have hurt him; but this would have involved an explanation, which she did not then care to give. So she contented herself with opening her gray eyes widely at the red-cheeked Mrs. Stidger—a fine specimen of Southwestern efflorescence—and then dismissed the subject altogether. The next day she wrote to her dearest friend in Boston: "I think I find the intoxicated portion of this community the least objectionable. I refer, my dear, to the men, of course. I do not know anything that could make the women tolerable."

In less than a week Miss Mary had forgotten this episode, except that her afternoon walks took thereafter, almost unconsciously, another direction. She noticed, however, that every morning a fresh cluster of azalea blossoms appeared among the flowers on her desk. This was not strange, as her little flock were aware of her fondness for flowers, and invariably kept her desk bright with anemones, syringas, and lupines; but on questioning them, they one and all professed ignorance of the azaleas. A few days later, Master Johnny Stidger, whose desk was nearest to the window, was suddenly taken with spasms of apparently gratuitous laughter that threatened the discipline of the school. All that Miss Mary could get from him was that someone had been "looking in the winder." Irate and indignant, she sallied from her hive to do battle with the intruder. As she turned the corner of the schoolhouse she came plump upon the quondam drunkard, now perfectly sober, and inexpressibly sheepish and guilty-looking.

These facts Miss Mary was not slow to take a feminine advantage of, in her present humor. But it was somewhat confusing to observe, also, that the beast, despite some faint signs of past dissipation, was amiable-looking—in fact, a kind of blond Samson, whose corn-colored silken beard apparently had never yet known the touch of barber's razor or Delilah's shears. So that the cutting speech which quivered on her ready tongue died upon her lips, and she contented herself with receiving his stammering apology with supercilious eyelids and the gathered skirts of uncontamination. When she re-entered the school-room, her eyes fell upon the azaleas with a new sense of revelation; and then she laughed, and the little people all laughed, and they were all unconsciously very happy.

It was a hot day, and not long after this, that two short-legged boys came to grief on the threshold of the school with a pail of water, which they had laboriously brought from the spring, and that Miss Mary compassionately seized the pail and started for the spring herself. At the foot of the hill a shadow crossed her path, and a blue-shirted arm dexterously but gently relieved her of her burden. Miss Mary was both embarrassed and angry. "If you carried more of that for yourself," she said spitefully to the blue arm, without deigning to raise her lashes to its owner, "you'd do better." In the submissive silence that followed she regretted the speech, and thanked him so sweetly at the door that he stumbled. Which caused the children to laugh again—a laugh in which Miss Mary joined, until the color came faintly into her pale cheek. The next day a barrel was mysteriously placed beside the door, and as mysteriously filled with fresh spring-water every morning.

Nor was this superior young person without other quiet attentions. "Profane Bill," driver of the Slumgullion Stage, widely known in the newspapers for his "gallantry" in invariably offering the box seat to the fair sex, had excepted Miss Mary from this attention, on the ground that he had a habit of "cussin' on up-grades," and gave her half the coach to herself. Jack Hamlin, a gambler, having once silently ridden with her in the same coach, afterward threw a decanter at the head of a confederate for mentioning her name in a barroom. The over-dressed mother of a pupil whose paternity was doubtful had often lingered near this astute vestal's temple, never daring to enter its sacred precincts, but content to worship the priestess from afar.

With such unconscious intervals the monotonous procession of blue skies, glittering sunshine, brief twilights, and starlit nights passed over Red Gulch. Miss Mary grew fond of walking in the sedate and proper woods. Perhaps she believed, with Mrs. Stidger, that the balsamic odors of the firs "did her chest good," for certainly her slight cough was less frequent and her step was firmer; perhaps she had learned the unending lesson which the patient pines are never weary of repeating to heedful or listless ears. And so one day she planned a picnic on Buckeye Hill, and took the children with her. Away from the dusty road, the straggling shanties, the yellow ditches, the clamor of restless engines, the cheap finery of shop windows, the deeper glitter of paint and colored glass, and the thin veneering which barbarism takes upon itself in such localities, what infinite relief was theirs! The last heap of ragged rock and clay passed, the last unsightly chasm crossed—how the waiting woods opened their long files to receive them! How the children—perhaps because they had not yet grown quite away from the breast of the bounteous Mother—threw themselves face downward on her brown bosom with uncouth caresses, filling the air with their laughter; and how Miss Mary herself—felinely fastidious and intrenched as she was in the purity of spotless skirts, collar, and cuffs—forgot all, and ran like a crested quail at the head of her brood, until, romping, laughing, and panting, with a loosened braid of brown hair, a hat hanging by a knotted ribbon from her throat, she came suddenly and violently, in the heart of the forest, upon the luckless Sandy!

The explanations, apologies, and not overwise conversation that ensued need not be indicated here. It would seem, however, that Miss Mary had already established some acquaintance with this ex-drunkard. Enough that he was soon accepted as one of the party; that the children, with that quick intelligence which Providence gives the helpless, recognized a friend, and played with his blond beard and long silken mustache, and took other liberties—as the helpless are apt to do. And when he had built a fire against a tree, and had shown them other mysteries of woodcraft, their admiration knew no bounds. At the close of two such foolish, idle, happy hours he found himself lying at the feet of the schoolmistress, gazing dreamily in her face as she sat upon the sloping hillside weaving wreaths of laurel and syringa, in very much the same attitude as he had lain when first they met. Nor was the similitude greatly forced. The weakness of an easy, sensuous nature, that had found a dreamy exaltation in liquor, it is to be feared was now finding an equal intoxication in love.

I think that Sandy was dimly conscious of this himself. I know that he longed to be doing something—slaying a grizzly, scalping a savage, or sacrificing himself in some way for the sake of this sallow-faced, gray-eyed schoolmistress. As I should like to present him in an heroic attitude, I stay my hand with great difficulty at this moment, being only withheld from introducing such an episode by a strong conviction that it does not usually occur at such times. And I trust that my fairest reader, who remembers that in a real crisis it is always some uninteresting stranger or unromantic policeman, and not Adolphus, who rescues, will forgive the omission.

So they sat there undisturbed—the woodpeckers chattering overhead and the voices of the children coming pleasantly from the hollow below. What they said matters little. What they thought—which might have been interesting—did not transpire. The woodpeckers only learned how Miss Mary was an orphan; how she left her uncle's house to come to California for the sake of health and independence; how Sandy was an orphan too; how he came to California for excitement; how he had lived a wild life, and how he was trying to reform; and other details, which from a woodpecker's viewpoint undoubtedly must have seemed stupid and a waste of time. But even in such trifles was the afternoon spent; and when the children were again gathered, and Sandy, with a delicacy which the schoolmistress well understood, took leave of them quietly at the outskirts of the settlement, it had seemed the shortest day of her weary life.

As the long, dry summer withered to its roots, the school term of Red Gulch—to use a local euphuism —"dried up" also. In another day Miss Mary would be free, and for a season, at least, Red Gulch would know her no more. She was seated alone in the schoolhouse, her cheek resting on her hand, her eyes half closed in one of those daydreams in which Miss Mary, I fear, to the danger of school discipline, was lately in the habit of indulging. Her lap was full of mosses, ferns, and other woodland memories. She was so preoccupied with these and her own thoughts that a gentle tapping at the door passed unheard, or translated itself into the remembrance of far-off woodpeckers. When at last it asserted itself more distinctly, she started up with a flushed cheek and opened the door. On the threshold stood a woman, the self-assertion and audacity of whose dress were in singular contrast to her timid, irresolute bearing.

Miss Mary recognized at a glance the dubious mother of her anonymous pupil. Perhaps she was disappointed, perhaps she was only fastidious; but as she coldly invited her to enter, she half unconsciously settled her white cuffs and collar, and gathered closer her own chaste skirts. It was, perhaps, for this reason that the embarrassed stranger, after a moment's hesitation, left her gorgeous parasol open and sticking in the dust beside the door, and then sat down at the farther end of a long bench. Her voice was husky as she began—

"I heerd tell that you were goin' down to the Bay tomorrow, and I couldn't let you go until I came to thank you for your kindness to my Tommy."

Tommy, Miss Mary said, was a good boy, and deserved more than the poor attention she could give him.

"Thank you, miss; thank ye!" cried the stranger, brightening even through the color which Red Gulch knew facetiously as her "war paint," and striving, in her embarrassment, to drag the long bench nearer the schoolmistress. "I thank you, miss, for that; and if I am his mother, there ain't a sweeter, dearer, better boy lives than him. And if I ain't much as says it, thar ain't a sweeter, dearer, angeler teacher lives than he's got."

Miss Mary, sitting primly behind her desk, with a ruler over her shoulder, opened her gray eyes widely at this, but said nothing.

"It ain't for you to be complimented by the like of me, I know," she went on hurriedly. "It ain't for me to be comin' here, in broad day, to do it, either; but I come to ask a favor—not for me, miss—not for me, but for the darling boy."

Encouraged by a look in the young school-mistress's eye, and putting her lilac-gloved hands together, the fingers downward, between her knees, she went on, in a low voice:

"You see, miss, there's no one the boy has any claim on but me, and I ain't the proper person to bring him up. I thought some last year of sending him away to Frisco to school, but when they talked of bringing a schoolma'am here, I waited till I saw you, and then I knew it was all right, and I could keep my boy a little longer. And, oh! miss, he loves you so much; and if you could hear him talk about you in his pretty way, and if he could ask you what I ask you now, you couldn't refuse him.

"It is natural," she went on rapidly, in a voice that trembled strangely between pride and humility—"it's natural that he should take to you, miss, for his father, when I first knew him, was a gentleman—and the boy must forget me, sooner or later—and so I ain't a-goin' to cry about that. For I come to ask you to take my Tommy—God bless him for the bestest, sweetest boy that lives—to—to—take him with you."

She had risen and caught the young girl's hand in her own, and had fallen on her knees beside her.

"I've money plenty, and it's all yours and his. Put him in some good school, where you can go and see him, and help him to—to—to forget his mother. Do with him what you like. The worst you can do will be kindness to what he will learn with me. Only take him out of this wicked life, this cruel place, this home of shame and sorrow. You will! I know you will—won't you? You will—you must not, you cannot say no! You will make him as pure, as gentle as yourself; and when he has grown up, you will tell him his father's name —the name that hasn't passed my lips for years—the name of Alexander Morton, whom they call here Sandy! Miss Mary!—do not take your hand away! Miss Mary, speak to me! You will take my boy? Do not put your face from me. I know it ought not to look on such as me. Miss Mary!—my God, be merciful!— she is leaving me!"

Miss Mary had risen, and in the gathering twilight, had felt her way to the open window. She stood there, leaning against the casement, her eyes fixed on the last rosy tints that were fading from the western sky. There was still some of its light on her pure young forehead, on her white collar, on her clasped white hands, but all fading slowly away. The suppliant had dragged herself, still on her knees, beside her.

"I know it takes time to consider. I will wait here all night; but I cannot go until you speak. Do not deny me now. You will!—I see it in your sweet face— such a face as I have seen in my dreams. I see it in your eyes, Miss Mary!—you will take my boy!"

The last red beam crept higher, suffused Miss

Mary's eyes with something of its glory, flickered, and faded, and went out. The sun had set on Red Gulch. In the twilight and silence Miss Mary's voice sounded pleasantly.

"I will take the boy. Send him to me tonight."

The happy mother raised the hem of Miss Mary's skirts to her lips. She would have buried her hot face in its virgin folds, but she dared not. She rose to her feet.

"Does—this man—know of your intention?" asked Miss Mary suddenly.

"No, nor cares. He has never even seen the child to know it."

"Go to him at once—tonight—now! Tell him what you have done. Tell him I have taken his child, and tell him—he must never see—see—the child again. Wherever it may be, he must not come; wherever I may take it, he must not follow! There, go now, please —I'm weary, and—have much yet to do!"

They walked together to the door. On the threshold the woman turned.

"Good night!"

She would have fallen at Miss Mary's feet. But at the same moment the young girl reached out her arms, caught the sinful woman to her own pure breast for one brief moment, and then closed and locked the door.

It was with a sudden sense of great responsibility that Profane Bill took the reins of the Slumgullion stage the next morning, for the schoolmistress was one of his passengers. As he entered the highroad, in obedience to a pleasant voice from the "inside," he suddenly reined up his horses and respectfully waited, as

Tommy hopped out at the command of Miss Mary.

"Not that bush, Tommy—the next."

Tommy whipped out his new pocketknife, and cutting a branch from a tall azalea bush, returned with it to Miss Mary.

"All right now?"

"All right!"

And the stage-door closed on the Idyl of Red Gulch.

BROWN OF CALAVERAS

A subdued tone of conversation, and the absence of cigar smoke and boot heels at the windows of the Wingdam stagecoach, made it evident that one of the inside passengers was a woman. A disposition on the part of loungers at the stations to congregate before the window, and some concern in regard to the appearance of coats, hats, and collars, further indicated that she was lovely. All of which Mr. Jack Hamlin, on the box-seat, noted with the smile of cynical philosophy. Not that he depreciated the sex, but that he recognized therein a deceitful element, the pursuit of which sometimes drew mankind away from the equally uncertain blandishments of poker—of which it may be remarked that Mr. Hamlin was a professional exponent.

So that when he placed his narrow boot on the wheel and leaped down he did not even glance at the window from which a green veil was fluttering, but lounged up and down with that listless and grave indifference of his class, which was, perhaps, the next thing to good breeding. With his closely buttoned figure and self-contained air he was a marked contrast to the other passengers, with their feverish restlessness and boisterous emotion; and even Bill Masters, a graduate of Harvard, with his slovenly dress, his overflowing vitality, his intense appreciation of lawlessness and barbarism, and his mouth filled with crackers and cheese, I fear cut but an unromantic figure beside this lonely calculator of chances, with his pale Greek face and Homeric gravity.

The driver called "All aboard!" and Mr. Hamlin returned to the coach. His foot was upon the wheel, and his face raised to the level of the open window, when, at the same moment, what appeared to him to be the finest eyes in the world suddenly met his. He quietly dropped down again, addressed a few words to one of the inside passengers, effected an exchange of seats, and as quietly took his place inside. Mr. Hamlin never allowed his philosophy to interfere with decisive and prompt action.

I fear that this irruption of Jack cast some restraint upon the other passengers, particularly those who were making themselves most agreeable to the lady. One of them leaned forward, and apparently conveyed to her information regarding Mr. Hamlin's profession in a single epithet. Whether Mr. Hamlin heard it, or whether he recognized in the informant a distinguished jurist, from whom, but a few evenings before, he had won several thousand dollars, I cannot say. His colorless face betrayed no sign; his black eyes, quietly observant, glanced indifferently past the legal gentleman, and rested on the much more pleasing features of his neighbor. An Indian stocism—said to be an inheritance from his maternal ancestor—stood him in good service, until the rolling wheels rattled upon the river gravel at Scott's Ferry, and the stage drew up at the International Hotel for dinner. The legal gentleman and a member of Congress leaped out, and stood ready to assist the descending goddess, while Colonel Starbottle of Siskiyou took charge of her parasol and shawl. In this multiplicity of attention there was a momentary confusion and delay. Jack Hamlin quietly opened the *opposite* door of the coach, took the lady's hand, with that decision and positiveness which a hesitating and undecided sex know how to admire, and in an instant had dexterously and gracefully swung her to the ground and again lifted her to the platform. An audible chuckle on the box, I fear, came from that other cynic, Yuba Bill, the driver. "Look keerfully arter that baggage, Kernel," said the expressman, with affected concern, as he looked after Colonel Starbottle, gloomily bringing up the rear of the triumphant procession to the waiting room.

Mr. Hamlin did not stay for dinner. His horse was already saddled and awaiting him. He dashed over the ford, up the gravelly hill, and out into the dusty perspective of the Wingdam road, like one leaving an unpleasant fancy behind him. The inmates of dusty cabins by the roadside shaded their eyes with their hands and looked after him, recognizing the man by his horse, and speculating what "was up with Comanche Jack." Yet much of this interest centered in the horse, in a community where the time made by "French Pete's" mare in his run from the Sheriff of Calaveras eclipsed all concern in the ultimate fate of that worthy.

The sweating flanks of his gray at length recalled him to himself. He checked his speed, and turning into a byroad sometimes used as a cutoff, trotted leisurely along, the reins hanging listlessly from his fingers. As he rode on, the character of the landscape changed and became more pastoral. Openings in groves of pine and sycamore disclosed some rude attempts at cultivation—a flowering vine trailed over the porch of one cabin, and a woman rocked her cradled babe under the roses of another. A little farther on, Mr. Hamlin came upon some barelegged children wading in the willowy creek, and so wrought upon them with a badinage peculiar to himself that they were emboldened to climb up his horse's legs and over his saddle, until he was fain to develop an exaggerated ferocity of demeanor, and to escape, leaving behind some kisses and coin. And then, advancing deeper into the woods, where all signs of habitation failed, he began to sing, uplifting a tenor so singularly sweet, and shaded by a pathos so subdued and tender, that I wot the robins and linnets stopped to listen. Mr. Hamlin's voice was not cultivated; the subject of his song was some sentimental lunacy, borrowed from the negro minstrels; but there thrilled through all some occult quality of tone and expression that was unspeakably touching. Indeed, it was a wonderful sight to see this sentimental blackleg, with a pack of cards in his pocket and a revolver at his back, sending his voice before him through the dim woods with a plaint about his "Nelly's grave," in a way that overflowed the eyes of the listener. A sparrow hawk, fresh from his sixth victim, possibly recognizing in Mr. Hamlin a kindred spirit, stared at him in surprise, and was fain to confess the superiority of man. With a superior predatory capacity *he* couldn't sing.

But Mr. Hamlin presently found himself again on the highroad and at his former pace. Ditches and banks of gravel, denuded hillsides, stumps, and decayed trunks of trees, took the place of woodland and ravine, and indicated his approach to civilization. Then a church steeple came in sight, and he knew that he had reached home. In a few moments he was clattering down the single narrow street that lost itself in a chaotic ruin of races, ditches, and tailings at the foot of the hill, and dismounted before the gilded windows of the Magnolia saloon. Passing through the long barroom, he pushed open a green baize door, entered a dark passage, opened another door with a passkey, and found himself in a dimly lighted room, whose furniture, though elegant and costly for the locality, showed signs of abuse. The inlaid center table was overlaid with stained disks that were not contemplated in the original design, the embroidered armchairs were discolored, and the green velvet lounge, on which Mr. Hamlin threw himself, was soiled at the foot with the red soil of Wingdam.

Mr. Hamlin did not sing in his cage. He lay still, looking at a highly colored painting above him, representing a young creature of opulent charms. It occurred to him then, for the first time, that he had never seen exactly that kind of a woman, and that, if he should, he would not probably fall in love with her. Perhaps he was thinking of another style of beauty. But just then someone knocked at the door. Without rising, he pulled a cord that apparently shot back a bolt, for the door swung open, and a man entered.

The newcomer was broad-shouldered and robust —a vigor not borne out in the face, which, though handsome, was singularly weak and disfigured by dissipation. He appeared to be, also, under the influence of liquor, for he started on seeing Mr. Hamlin, and said, "I thought Kate was here"; stammered, and seemed confused and embarrassed.

Mr. Hamlin smiled the smile which he had before worn on the Wingdam coach, and sat up, quite refreshed and ready for business.

"You didn't come up on the stage," continued the newcomer, "did you?"

"No," replied Hamlin; "I left it at Scott's Ferry. It isn't due for half an hour yet. But how's luck, Brown?"

"D—d bad," said Brown, his face suddenly assuming an expression of weak despair. "I'm cleaned out again, Jack," he continued, in a whining tone, that formed a pitiable contrast to his bulky figure; "can't you help me with a hundred till tomorrow's cleanup? You see I've got to send money home to the old woman, and—you've won twenty times that amount from me."

The conclusion was, perhaps, not entirely logical, but Jack overlooked it, and handed the sum to his visitor. "The old-woman business is about played out, Brown," he added, by way of commentary; "why don't you say you want to buck ag'in' faro? You know you ain't married!"

"Fact, sir," said Brown, with a sudden gravity, as if the mere contact of the gold with the palm of the hand had imparted some dignity to his frame. "I've got a wife—a d—d good one, too, if I do say it—in the States. It's three years since I've seen her, and a year since I've writ to her. When things is about straight, and we get down to the lead, I'm going to send for her."

"And Kate?" queried Mr. Hamlin, with his previous smile.

Mr. Brown of Calaveras essayed an archness of glance to cover his confusion, which his weak face and whiskey-muddled intellect but poorly carried out, and said—

"D—n it, Jack, a man must have a little liberty, you know. But come, what do you say to a little game? Give us a show to double this hundred."

Jack Hamlin looked curiously at his fatuous friend. Perhaps he knew that the man was predestined to lose the money, and preferred that it should flow back into his own coffers rather than any other. He nodded his head, and drew his chair toward the table. At the same moment there came a rap upon the door.

Mr. Hamlin shot back the bolt and the door opened. But, for the first time in his life, he staggered to his feet utterly unnerved and abashed, and for the first time in his life the hot blood crimsoned his colorless cheeks to his forehead. For before him stood the lady he had lifted from the Wingdam coach, whom Brown, dropping his cards with a hysterical laugh, greeted as—

"My old woman, by thunder!"

They say that Mrs. Brown burst into tears and reproaches of her husband. I saw her in 1857 at Marysville, and disbelieve the story. And the *Wingdam Chronicle* of the next week, under the head of "Touching Reunion," said: "One of those beautiful and touching incidents peculiar to California life occurred last week in our city. The wife of one of Wingdam's eminent pioneers, tired of the effete civilization of the East and its inhospitable climate, resolved to join her noble husband upon these golden shores. Without informing him of her intention, she undertook the long journey, and arrived last week. The joy of the husband may be easier imagined than described. The meeting is said to have been indescribably affecting. We trust her example may be followed."

Whether owing to Mrs. Brown's influence, or to some more successful speculations, Mr. Brown's financial fortune from that day steadily improved. He bought out his partners in the "Nip and Tuck" lead, with money which was said to have been won at poker a week or two after his wife's arrival, but which rumor, adopting Mrs. Brown's theory that Brown had forsworn the gaming table, declared to have been furnished by Mr. Jack Hamlin. He built and furnished the Wingdam House, which pretty Mrs. Brown's great popularity kept overflowing with guests. He was elected to the Assembly, and gave largess to churches. A street in Wingdam was named in his honor.

Yet it was noted that in proportion as he waxed wealthy and fortunate, he grew pale, thin, and anxious. As his wife's popularity increased, he became fretful and impatient. The most uxorious of husbands, he was absurdly jealous. If he did not interfere with his wife's social liberty, it was because it was maliciously whispered that his first and only attempt was met by an outburst from Mrs. Brown that terrified him into silence. Much of this kind of gossip came from those of her own sex whom she had supplanted in the chivalrous attentions of Wingdam, which, like most popular chivalry, was devoted to an admiration of power, whether of masculine force or feminine beauty. It should be remembered, too, in her extenuation, that since her arrival she had been the unconscious priestess of a mythological worship, perhaps not more ennobling to her womanhood than that which distinguished an older Greek democracy. I think that Brown was dimly conscious of this. But his only confidant was Jack Hamlin, whose infelix reputation naturally precluded any open intimacy with the family, and whose visits were infrequent.

It was midsummer and a moonlit night, and Mrs. Brown, very rosy, large-eyed, and pretty, sat upon the piazza, enjoying the fresh incense of the mountain breeze, and, it is to be freared, another incense which was not so fresh nor quite as innocent. Beside her sat Colonel Starbottle and Judge Boompointer, and a later addition to her court in the shape of a foreign tourist. She was in good spirits.

"What do you see down the road?" inquired the gallant Colonel, who had been conscious for the last few minutes that Mrs. Brown's attention was diverted.

"Dust," said Mrs. Brown, with a sigh. "Only Sister Anne's 'flock of sheep.' "

The Colonel, whose literary recollections did not extend farther back than last week's paper, took a more practical view. "It ain't sheep," he continued; "it's a horseman. Judge, ain't that Jack Hamlin's gray?"

But the Judge didn't know; and as Mrs. Brown suggested the air was growing too cold for further investigations, they retired to the parlor.

Mr. Brown was in the stable, where he generally retired after dinner. Perhaps it was to show his contempt for his wife's companions; perhaps, like other weak natures, he found pleasure in the exercise of absolute power over inferior animals. He had a certain gratification in the training of a chestnut mare, whom he could beat or caress as pleased him, which he couldn't do with Mrs. Brown. It was here that he recognized a certain gray horse which had just come in, and looking a little farther on, found his rider. Brown's greeting was cordial and hearty; Mr. Hamlin's somewhat restrained. But, at Brown's urgent request, he followed him up the back stairs to a narrow corridor, and thence to a small room looking out upon the stable yard. It was plainly furnished with a bed, a table, a few chairs, and a rack for guns and whips.

"This yer's my home, Jack," said Brown with a sigh, as he threw himself upon the bed and motioned his companion to a chair. "Her room's t' other end of the hall. It's more'n six months since we've lived together, or met, except at meals. It's mighty rough papers on the head of the house, ain't it?" he said with a forced laugh. "But I'm glad to see you, Jack, d—d glad," and he reached from the bed, and again shook the unresponsive hand of Jack Hamlin.

"I brought ye up here, for I didn't want to talk in the stable; though, for the matter of that, it's all round town. Don't strike a light. We can talk here in the moonshine. Put up your feet on that winder and sit here beside me. Thar's whiskey in that jug."

Mr. Hamlin did not avail himself of the information. Brown of Calaveras turned his face to the wall, and continued—

"If I didn't love the woman, Jack, I wouldn't mind. But it's loving her, and seeing her day arter day goin' on at this rate, and no one to put down the brake; that's what gits me! But I'm glad to see ye, Jack, d—d glad."

In the darkness he groped about until he had found and wrung his companion's hand again. He would have detained it, but Jack slipped it into the buttoned breast of his coat, and asked listlessly, "How long has this been going on?"

"Ever since she came here; ever since the day she walked into the Magnolia. I was a fool then; Jack, I'm a fool now; but I didn't know how much I loved her till then. And she hasn't been the same woman since.

"But that ain't all, Jack; and it's what I wanted to see you about, and I'm glad you've come. It ain't that she doesn't love me any more; it ain't that she fools with every chap that comes along; for perhaps I staked her love and lost it, as I did everything else at the Magnolia; and perhaps foolin' is nateral to some women, and thar ain't no great harm done, 'cept to the fools. But, Jack, I think—I think she loves somebody else. Don't move, Jack! don't move; if your pistol hurts ye, take it off.

'It's been more'n six months now that she's seemed unhappy and lonesome, and kinder nervous and scared-like. And sometimes I've ketched her lookin' at me sort of timid and pitying. And she writes to somebody. And for the last week she's been gathering

her own things—trinkets, and furbelows, and jew'lry
—and, Jack, I think she's goin' off. I could stand all
but that. To have her steal away like a thief!" He put
his face downward to the pillow, and for a few moments there was no sound but the ticking of a clock on
the mantel. Mr. Hamlin lit a cigar, and moved to the
open window. The moon no longer shone into the
room, and the bed and its occupant were in shadow.
"What shall I do, Jack?" said the voice from the darkness.

The answer came promptly and clearly from the
window side, "Spot the man, and kill him on sight."

"But, Jack"—

"He's took the risk!"

"But will that bring *her* back?"

Jack did not reply, but moved from the window towards the door.

"Don't go yet, Jack; light the candle and sit by the
table. It's a comfort to see ye, if nothin' else."

Jack hesitated and then complied. He drew a pack
of cards from his pocket and shuffled them, glancing
at the bed. But Brown's face was turned to the wall.
When Mr. Hamlin had shuffled the cards, he cut
them, and dealt one card on the opposite side of the
table towards the bed, and another on his side of
the table for himself. The first was a deuce; his own
card a king. He then shuffled and cut again. This
time "dummy" had a queen and himself a four-spot.
Jack brightened up for the third deal. It brought his
adversary a deuce and himself a king again. "Two out
of three," said Jack audibly.

"What's that, Jack?" said Brown.

"Nothing."

Then Jack tried his hand with dice; but he always threw sixes and his imaginary opponent aces. The force of habit is sometimes confusing.

Meanwhile some magnetic influence in Mr. Hamlin's presence, or the anodyne of liquor, or both, brought surcease of sorrow, and Brown slept. Mr. Hamlin moved his chair to the window and looked out on the town of Wingdam, now sleeping peacefully, its harsh outlines softened and subdued, its glaring colors mellowed and sobered in the moonlight that flowed over all. In the hush he could hear the gurgling of water in the ditches and the sighing of the pines beyond the hill. Then he looked up at the firmament, and as he did so a star shot across the twinkling field. Presently another, and then another. The phenomenon suggested to Mr. Hamlin a fresh augury. If in another fifteen minutes another star should fall— He sat there, watch in hand, for twice that time, but the phenomenon was not repeated.

The clock struck two, and Brown still slept. Mr. Hamlin approached the table and took from his pocket a letter, which he read by the flickering candlelight. It contained only a single line, written in pencil, in a woman's hand—

"Be at the corral with the buggy at three."

The sleeper moved uneasily and then awoke. "Are you there, Jack?"

"Yes."

"Don't go yet. I dreamed just now, Jack—dreamed of old times. I thought that Sue and me was being married agin, and that the parson, Jack, was—who do you think?—you!"

The gambler laughed, and seated himself on the bed, the paper still in his hand.

"It's a good sign, ain't it?" queried Brown.

"I reckon! Say, old man, hadn't you better get up?"

The "old man," thus affectionately appealed to, rose, with the assistance of Hamlin's outstretched hand.

"Smoke?"

Brown mechanically took the proffered cigar.

"Light?"

Jack had twisted the letter into a spiral, lit it, and held it for his companion. He continued to hold it until it was consumed, and dropped the fragment—a fiery star—from the open window. He watched it as it fell, and then returned to his friend.

"Old man," he said, placing his hands upon Brown's shoulders, "in ten minutes I'll be on the road, and gone like that spark. We won't see each other agin; but, before I go, take a fool's advice: sell out all you've got, take your wife with you, and quit the country. It ain't no place for you nor her. Tell her she must go; make her go if she won't. Don't whine because you can't be a saint and she ain't an angel. Be a man, and treat her like a woman. Don't be a d—d fool. Good-by."

He tore himself from Brown's grasp and leaped down the stairs like a deer. At the stable door he collared the half-sleeping hostler, and backed him against the wall. "Saddle my horse in two minutes, or I'll"— The ellipsis was frightfully suggestive.

"The missis said you was to have the buggy," stammered the man.

"D—n the buggy!"

The horse was saddled as fast as the nervous hands of the astounded hostler could manipulate buckle and strap.

"Is anything up, Mr. Hamlin?" said the man, who, like all his class, admired the *élan* of his fiery patron, and was really concerned in his welfare.

"Stand aside!"

The man fell back. With an oath, a bound, and clatter, Jack was into the road. In another moment, to the man's half-awakened eyes, he was but a moving cloud of dust in the distance, towards which a star just loosed from its brethren was trailing a stream of fire.

But early that morning the dwellers by the Wingdam turnpike, miles away, heard a voice, pure as a skylark's, singing afield. They who were asleep turned over on their rude couches to dream of youth, and love, and olden days. Hard-faced men and anxious gold-seekers, already at work, ceased their labors and leaned upon their picks to listen to a romantic vagabond ambling away against the rosy sunrise.

SALOMY JANE'S KISS

Only one shot had been fired. It had gone wide of its mark,—the ringleader of the Vigilantes,—and had left Red Pete, who had fired it, covered by their rifles and at their mercy. For his hand had been cramped by hard riding, and his eye distracted by their sudden onset, and so the inevitable end had come. He submitted sullenly to his captors; his companion fugitive and horse-thief gave up the protracted struggle with a feeling not unlike relief. Even the hot and revengeful victors were content. They had taken their men alive. At any time during the long chase they could have brought them down by a rifle-shot, but it would have been unsportsmanlike, and have ended in a free fight, instead of an example. And, for the matter of that, their doom was already sealed. Their end, by a rope and a tree, although not sanctified by law, would have at least the deliberation of justice. It was the tribute paid by the Vigilantes to that order which they had themselves disregarded in the pursuit and capture. Yet this strange logic of the frontier sufficed them, and gave a certain dignity to the climax.

"Ef you've got anything to say to your folks, say it *now*, and say it quick," said the ringleader.

Red Pete glanced around him. He had been run to earth at his own cabin in the clearing, whence a few relations and friends, mostly women and children, non-combatants, had outflowed, gazing vacantly at the twenty Vigilantes who surrounded them. All were accustomed to scenes of violence, blood-feud, chase, and hardship; it was only the suddenness of the onset and its quick result that had surprised them. They looked on with dazed curiosity and some disappointment; there had been no fight to speak of—no spectacle! A boy, nephew of Red Pete, got upon the rain-barrel to view the proceedings more comfortably; a tall, handsome, lazy Kentucky girl, a visiting neighbor, leaned against the doorpost, chewing gum. Only a yellow hound was actively perplexed. He could not make out if a hunt were just over or beginning, and ran eagerly backwards and forwards, leaping alternately upon the captives and the captors.

The ringleader repeated his challenge. Red Pete gave a reckless laugh and looked at his wife.

At which Mrs. Red Pete came forward. It seemed that she had much to say, incoherently, furiously, vindictively, to the ringleader. His soul would roast in hell for that day's work! He called himself a man, skunkin' in the open and afraid to show himself except with a crowd of other "Kiyi's" around a house of women and children. Heaping insult upon insult, inveighing against his low blood, his ancestors, his dubious origin, she at last flung out a wild taunt of his invalid wife, the insult of a woman to a woman, until his white face grew rigid, and only that Western-

American fetich of the sanctity of sex kept his twitching fingers from the lock of his rifle. Even her husband noticed it, and with a half-authoritative "Let up on that, old gal," and a pat of his freed left hand on her back, took his last parting. The ringleader, still white under the lash of the woman's tongue, turned abruptly to the second captive. "And if *you've* got anybody to say 'good-by' to, now's your chance."

The man looked up. Nobody stirred or spoke. He was a stranger there, being a chance confederate picked up by Red Pete, and known to no one. Still young, but an outlaw from his abandoned boyhood, of which father and mother were only a forgotten dream, he loved horses and stole them, fully accepting the frontier penalty of life for the interference with that animal on which a man's life so often depended. But he understood the good points of a horse, as was shown by the one he bestrode—until a few days before the property of Judge Boompointer. This was his sole distinction.

The unexpected question stirred him for a moment out of the attitude of reckless indifference, for attitude it was, and a part of his profession. But it may have touched him that at that moment he was less than his companion and his virago wife. However, he only shook his head. As he did so his eye casually fell on the handsome girl by the doorpost, who was looking at him. The ringleader, too, may have been touched by his complete loneliness, for *he* hesitated. At the same moment he saw that the girl was looking at his friendless captive.

A grotesque idea struck him.

"Salomy Jane, ye might do worse than come yere

and say 'good-by' to a dying man, and him a
stranger," he said.

There seemed to be a subtle stroke of poetry and
irony in this that equally struck the apathetic crowd.
It was well known that Salomy Jane Clay thought no
small potatoes of herself, and always held off the local
swain with a lazy, nymph-like scorn. Nevertheless, she
slowly disengaged herself from the doorpost, and, to
everybody's astonishment, lounged with languid grace
and outstretched hand towards the prisoner. The color
came into the gray, reckless mask which the doomed
man wore as her right hand grasped his left, just
loosed by his captors. Then she paused; her shy,
fawn-like eyes grew bold, and fixed themselves upon
him. She took the chewing-gum from her mouth,
wiped her red lips with the back of her hand, by a sudden lithe spring placed her foot on his stirrup, and,
bounding to the saddle, threw her arms about his neck
and pressed a kiss upon his lips.

They remained thus for a hushed moment—the
man on the threshold of death, the young woman in
the fullness of youth and beauty—linked together.
Then the crowd laughed; in the audacious effrontery
of the girl's act the ultimate fate of the two men was
forgotten. She slipped languidly to the ground; *she*
was the focus of all eyes,—she only! The ringleader
saw it and his opportunity. He shouted: "Time's up!
Forward!" urged his horse beside his captives, and the
next moment the whole cavalcade was sweeping over
the clearing into the darkening woods.

Their destination was Sawyer's Crossing, the head-
quarters of the committee, where the council was still
sitting, and where both culprits were to expiate the

offense of which that council had already found them guilty. They rode in great and breathless haste,—a haste in which, strangely enough, even the captives seemed to join. That haste possibly prevented them from noticing the singular change which had taken place in the second captive since the episode of the kiss. His high color remained, as if it had burned through his mask of indifference; his eyes were quick, alert, and keen, his mouth half open as if the girl's kiss still lingered there. And that haste had made them careless, for the horse of the man who led him slipped in a gopher-hole, rolled over, unseated his rider, and even dragged the bound and helpless second captive from Judge Boompointer's favorite mare. In an instant they were all on their feet again, but in that supreme moment the second captive felt the cords which bound his arms had slipped to his wrists. By keeping his elbows to his sides, and obliging the others to help him mount, it escaped their notice. By riding close to his captors, and keeping in the crush of the throng, he further concealed the accident, slowly working his hands downwards out of his bonds.

Their way lay through a sylvan wilderness, mid-leg deep in ferns, whose tall fronds brushed their horses' sides in their furious gallop and concealed the flapping of the captive's loosened cords. The peaceful vista, more suggestive of the offerings of nymph and shepherd than of human sacrifice, was in a strange contrast to this whirlwind rush of stern, armed men. The westering sun pierced the subdued light and the tremor of leaves with yellow lances; birds started into song on blue and dove-like wings, and on either side of the trail of this vengeful storm could be heard the murmur of hidden and tranquil waters. In a few moments they would be on the open ridge, whence sloped the common turnpike to "Sawyer's," a mile away. It was the custom of returning cavalcades to take this hill at headlong speed, with shouts and cries that heralded their coming. They withheld the latter that day, as inconsistent with their dignity; but, emerging from the wood, swept silently like an avalanche down the slope. They were well under way, looking only to their horses, when the second captive slipped his right arm from the bonds and succeeded in grasping the reins that lay trailing on the horse's neck. A sudden vaquero jerk, which the well-trained animal understood, threw him on his haunches with his forelegs firmly planted on the slope. The rest of the cavalcade swept on; the man who was leading the captive's horse by the riata, thinking only of another accident, dropped the line to save himself from being dragged backwards from his horse. The captive wheeled, and the next moment was galloping furiously up the slope.

  It was the work of a moment; a trained horse and an experienced hand. The cavalcade had covered nearly fifty yards before they could pull up; the freed captive had covered half that distance uphill. The road was so narrow that only two shots could be fired, and these broke dust two yards ahead of the fugitive. They had not dared to fire low; the horse was the more valuable animal. The fugitive knew this in his extremity also, and would have gladly taken a shot in his own leg to spare that of his horse. Five men were detached to recapture or kill him. The latter seemed inevitable. But he had calculated his chances; before they could reload he had reached the woods again;

winding in and out between the pillared tree trunks, he offered no mark. They knew his horse was superior to their own; at the end of two hours they returned, for he had disappeared without track or trail. The end was briefly told in the "Sierra Record:"—

"Red Pete, the notorious horse-thief, who had so long eluded justice, was captured and hung by the Sawyer's Crossing Vigilantes last week; his confederate, unfortunately, escaped on a valuable horse belonging to Judge Boompointer. The judge had refused one thousand dollars for the horse only a week before. As the thief, who is still at large, would find it difficult to dispose of so valuable an animal without detection, the chances are against either of them turning up again."

Salomy Jane watched the cavalcade until it had disappeared. Then she became aware that her brief popularity had passed. Mrs. Red Pete, in stormy hysterics, had included her in a sweeping denunciation of the whole universe, possibly for simulating an emotion in which she herself was deficient. The other women hated her for her momentary exaltation above them; only the children still admired her as one who had undoubtedly "canoodled" with a man "a-going to be hung"—a daring flight beyond their wildest ambition. Salomy Jane accepted the change with charming unconcern. She put on her yellow nankeen sunbonnet, —a hideous affair that would have ruined any other woman, but which only enhanced the piquancy of her fresh brunette skin,—tied the strings, letting the blue-black braids escape below its frilled curtain behind, jumped on her mustang with a casual display of agile ankles in shapely white stockings, whistled to the hound, and waving her hand with a "So long, sonny!" to the lately bereft but admiring nephew, flapped and fluttered away in her short brown holland gown.

Her father's house was four miles distant. Contrasted with the cabin she had just quitted, it was a superior dwelling, with a long "lean-to" at the rear, which brought the eaves almost to the ground and made it look like a low triangle. It had a long barn and cattle sheds, for Madison Clay was a "great" stock-raiser and the owner of a "quarter section." It had a sitting-room and a parlor organ, whose transportation thither had been a marvel of "packing." These things were supposed to give Salomy Jane an undue importance, but the girl's reserve and inaccessibility to local advances were rather the result of a cool, lazy temperament and the preoccupation of a large, protecting admiration for her father, for some years a widower. For Mr. Madison Clay's life had been threatened in one or two feuds,—it was said, not without cause,—and it is possible that the pathetic spectacle of her father doing his visiting with a shotgun may have touched her closely and somewhat prejudiced her against the neighboring masculinity. The thought that cattle, horses, and "quarter section" would one day be hers did not disturb her calm. As for Mr. Clay, he accepted her as housewifely, though somewhat "interfering," and, being one of "his own womankind," therefore not without some degree of merit.

"Wot's this yer I'm hearin' of your doin's over at Red Pete's? Honeyfoglin' with a horse-thief, eh?", said Mr. Clay two days later at breakfast.

"I reckon you heard about the straight thing, then," said Salomy Jane unconcernedly, without looking round.

"What do you kalkilate Rube will say to it? What are you goin' to tell *him?*" said Mr. Clay sarcastically.

"Rube," or Reuben Waters, was a swain supposed to be favored particularly by Mr. Clay. Salomy Jane looked up.

"I'll tell him that when *he's* on his way to be hung, I'll kiss him,—not till then," said the young lady brightly.

This delightful witticism suited the paternal humor, and Mr. Clay smiled; but, nevertheless, he frowned a moment afterwards.

"But this yer hoss-thief got away arter all, and that's a hoss of a different color," he said grimly.

Salomy Jane put down her knife and fork. This was certainly a new and different phase of the situation. She had never thought of it before, and, strangely enough, for the first time she became interested in the man. "Got away?" she repeated. "Did they let him off?"

"Not much," said her father briefly. "Slipped his cords, and going down the grade pulled up short, just like a vaquero agin a lassoed bull, almost draggin' the man leadin' him off his hoss, and he skyuted up the grade. For that matter, on that hoss o' Judge Boompointer's he mout have dragged the whole posse of 'em down on their knees ef he liked! Sarved 'em right, too. Instead of stringin' him up afore the door, or shootin' him on sight, they must allow to take him down afore the hull committee 'for an example.' 'Example' be blowed! Ther' 's example enough when

some stranger comes unbeknownst slap onter a man
hanged to a tree and plugged full of holes. *That's* an
example, and *he* knows what it means. Wot more
do ye want? But then those Vigilantes is allus clingin'
and hangin' onter some mere scrap o' the law they're
pretendin' to despise. It makes me sick! Why, when
Jake Myers shot your ole Aunt Viney's second husband, and I laid in wait for Jake afterwards in the
Butternut Hollow, did *I* tie him to his hoss and fetch
him down to your Aunt Viney's cabin 'for an example' before I plugged him? No!" in deep disgust. "No!
Why, I just meandered through the woods, careless-
like, till he comes out, and I just rode up to him, and
I said"—

But Salomy Jane had heard her father's story before. Even one's dearest relatives are apt to become
tiresome in narration. "I know, Dad," she interrupted;
"but this yer man,—this hoss-thief,—did *he* get clean
away without gettin' hurt at all?"

"He did, and unless he's fool enough to sell the
hoss, he kin keep away, too. So ye see, ye can't ladle
out purp stuff about a 'dyin' stranger' to Rube. He
won't swaller it."

"All the same, Dad," returned the girl cheerfully,
"I reckon to say it, and say *more;* I'll tell him that ef
he manages to get away too, I'll marry him—there!
But ye don't ketch Rube takin' any such risks in gettin'
ketched, or in gettin' away arter!"

Madison Clay smiled grimly, pushed back his chair,
rose, dropped a perfunctory kiss on his daughter's
hair, and, taking his shotgun from the corner, departed on a peaceful Samaritan mission to a cow who
had dropped a calf in the far pasture. Inclined as he

was to Reuben's wooing from his eligibility as to
property, he was conscious that he was sadly deficient
in certain qualities inherent in the Clay family. It certainly would be a kind of *mésalliance*.

Left to herself, Salomy Jane stared a long while at
the coffeepot, and then called the two squaws who as-
sisted her in her household duties, to clear away the
things while she went up to her own room to make
her bed. Here she was confronted with a possible prospect of that proverbial bed she might be making in
her willfulness, and on which she must lie, in the pho-
tograph of a somewhat serious young man of refined
features—Reuben Waters—stuck in her window-
frame. Salomy Jane smiled over her last witticism regarding him and enjoyed it, like your true humorist,
and then, catching sight of her own handsome face in
the little mirror, smiled again. But wasn't it funny
about that horse-thief getting off after all? Good
Lordy! Fancy Reuben hearing he was alive and going
round with that kiss of hers set on his lips! She laughed
again, a little more abstractedly. And he had returned
it like a man, holding her tight and almost breathless,
and he going to be hung the next minute! Salomy Jane
had been kissed at other times, by force, chance, or
stratagem. In a certain ingenuous forfeit game of
the locality, known as "I'm apinin'," many had
"pined" for a "sweet kiss" from Salomy Jane, which
she had yielded in a sense of honor and fair play.
She had never been kissed like this before—she would
never again; and yet the man was alive! And behold,
she could see in the mirror that she was blushing!

She should hardly know him again. A young man
with very bright eyes, a flushed and sunburnt cheek,

a kind of fixed look in the face, and no beard; no, none that she could feel. Yet he was not at all like Reuben, not a bit. She took Reuben's picture from the window, and laid it on her workbox. And to think she did not even know this young man's name! That was queer. To be kissed by a man whom she might never know! Of course he knew hers. She wondered if he remembered it and her. But of course he was so glad to get off with his life that he never thought of anything else. Yet she did not give more than four or five minutes to these speculations, and, like a sensible girl, thought of something else. Once again, however, in opening the closet, she found the brown holland gown she had worn on the day before; thought it very unbecoming, and regretted that she had not worn her best gown on her visit to Red Pete's cottage. On such an occasion she really might have been more impressive.

When her father came home that night she asked him the news. No, they had *not* captured the second horse-thief, who was still at large. Judge Boompointer talked of invoking the aid of the despised law. It remained, then, to see whether the horse-thief was fool enough to try to get rid of the animal. Red Pete's body had been delivered to his widow. Perhaps it would only be neighborly for Salomy Jane to ride over to the funeral. But Salomy Jane did not take to the suggestion kindly, nor yet did she explain to her father that, as the other man was still living, she did not care to undergo a second disciplining at the widow's hands. Nevertheless, she contrasted her situation with that of the widow with a new and singular satisfaction. It might have been Red Pete who had escaped. But he had not the grit of the nameless one. She had already settled his heroic quality.

"Ye ain't harkenin' to me, Salomy."

Salomy Jane started.

"Here I'm askin' ye if ye've see that hound Phil Larrabee sneaking by yer to-day?"

Salomy Jane had not. But she became interested and self-reproachful, for she knew that Phil Larrabee was one of her father's enemies. "He wouldn't dare to go by here unless he knew you were out," she said quickly.

"That's what gets me," he said, scratching his grizzled head. "I've been kind o' thinkin' o' him all day, and one of them Chinamen said he saw him at Sawyer's Crossing. He was a kind of friend o' Pete's wife. That's why I thought yer might find out ef he'd been there." Salomy Jane grew more self-reproachful at her father's self-interest in her "neighborliness." "But that ain't all," continued Mr. Clay. "Thar was tracks over the far pasture that warn't mine. I followed them, and they went round and round the house two or three times, ez ef they mout hev bin prowlin', and then I lost 'em in the woods again. It's just like that sneakin' hound Larrabee to hev bin lyin' in wait for me and afraid to meet a man fair and square in the open."

"You just lie low, dad, for a day or two more, and let me do a little prowlin'," said the girl, with sympathetic indignation in her dark eyes. "Ef it's that skunk, I'll spot him soon enough and let you know whar he's hiding."

"You'll just stay where ye are, Salomy," said her father decisively. "This ain't no woman's work—

though I ain't sayin' you haven't got more head for it than some men I know."

Nevertheless, that night, after her father had gone to bed, Salomy Jane sat by the open window of the sitting-room in an apparent attitude of languid contemplation, but alert and intent of eye and ear. It was a fine moonlit night. Two pines near the door, solitary pickets of the serried ranks of distant forest, cast long shadows like paths to the cottage, and sighed their spiced breath in the windows. For there was no frivolity of vine or flower round Salomy Jane's bower. The clearing was too recent, the life too practical, for vanities like these. But the moon added a vague elusiveness to everything, softened the rigid outlines of the sheds, gave shadows to the lidless windows, and touched with merciful indirectness the hideous débris of refuse gravel and the gaunt scars of burnt vegetation before the door. Even Salomy Jane was affected by it, and exhaled something between a sigh and a yawn with the breath of the pines. Then she suddenly sat upright.

Her quick ear had caught a faint "click, click," in the direction of the wood; her quicker instinct and rustic training enabled her to determine that it was the ring of a horse's shoe on flinty ground; her knowledge of the locality told her it came from the spot where the trail passed over an outcrop of flint, scarcely a quarter of a mile from where she sat, and within the clearing. It was no errant "stock," for the foot was *shod* with iron; it was a mounted trespasser by night, and boded no good to a man like Clay.

She rose, threw her shawl over her head, more for disguise than shelter, and passed out of the door. A sudden impulse made her seize her father's shotgun

from the corner where it stood,—not that she feared
any danger to herself, but that it was an excuse. She
made directly for the wood, keeping in the shadow
of the pines as long as she could. At the fringe she
halted; whoever was there must pass her before reach-
ing the house.

Then there seemed to be a suspense of all nature.
Everything was deadly still—even the moonbeams
appeared no longer tremulous; soon there was a rus-
tle as of some stealthy animal among the ferns, and
then a dismounted man stepped into the moonlight.
It was the horse-thief—the man she had kissed!

For a wild moment a strange fancy seized her usually sane intellect and stirred her temperate blood.
The news they had told her was *not* true; he had been
hung, and this was his ghost! He looked as white and
spirit-like in the moonlight, dressed in the same
clothes, as when she saw him last. He had evidently
seen her approaching, and moved quickly to meet
her. But in his haste he stumbled slightly; she reflected
suddenly that ghosts did not stumble, and a feel
of relief came over her. And it was no assassin of her
father that had been prowling around—only this unhappy fugitive. A momentary color came into her
cheek; her coolness and hardihood returned; it was
with a tinge of sauciness in her voice that she said:—

"I reckoned you were a ghost."

"I mout have been," he said, looking at her fixedly;
"but I reckon I'd have come back here all the same."

"It's a little riskier comin' back alive," she said,
with a levity that died on her lips, for a singular nerv-
ousness, half fear and half expectation, was beginning
to take the place of her relief of a moment ago. "Then

it was *you* who was prowlin' round and makin'
tracks in the far pasture?"

"Yes; I came straight here when I got away."

She felt his eyes were burning her, but did not dare
to raise her own. "Why," she began, hesitated, and
ended vaguely. "*How* did you get here?"

"You helped me!"

"I?"

"Yes. That kiss you gave me put life into me—
gave me strength to get away. I swore to myself I'd
come back and thank you, alive or dead."

Every word he said she could have anticipated, so
plain the situation seemed to her now. And every word
he said she knew was the truth. Yet her cool common
sense struggled against it.

"What's the use of your escaping, ef you're comin'
back here to be ketched again?" she said pertly.

He drew a little nearer to her, but seemed to her the
more awkward as she resumed her self-possession.
His voice, too, was broken, as if by exhaustion, as he
said, catching his breath at intervals:—

"I'll tell you. You did more for me than you think.
You made another man o' me. I never had a man,
woman, or child do to me what you did. I never had a
friend—only a pal like Red Pete, who picked me up
'on shares.' I want to quit this yer—what I'm doin'. I
want to begin by doin' the square thing to you"— He
stopped, breathed hard, and then said brokenly, "My
hoss is over thar, staked out. I want to give him to you.
Judge Boompointer will give you a thousand dollars
for him. I ain't lyin'; it's God's truth! I saw it on the
handbill agin a tree. Take him, and I'll get away afoot.
Take him. It's the only thing I can do for you, and I

know it don't half pay for what you did. Take it; your
father can get a reward for you, if you can't."

Such were the ethics of this strange locality that neither the man who made the offer nor the girl to whom
it was made was struck by anything that seemed il-
logical or indelicate, or at all inconsistent with justice
or the horse-thief's real conversion. Salomy Jane nevertheless dissented, from another and weaker reason.

"I don't want your hoss, though I reckon dad
might; but you're just starvin'. I'll get suthin'." She
turned towards the house.

"Say you'll take the hoss first," he said, grasping
her hand. At the touch she felt herself coloring and
struggled, expecting perhaps another kiss. But he
dropped her hand. She turned again with a saucy gesture, said, "Hol' on; I'll come right back," and slipped
away, the mere shadow of a coy and flying nymph in
the moonlight, until she reached the house.

Here she not only procured food and whiskey, but
added a long dust-coat and hat of her father's to her
burden. They would serve as a disguise for him and
hide that heroic figure, which she thought everybody
must now know as she did. Then she rejoined him
breathlessly. But he put the food and whiskey aside.

"Listen," he said; "I've turned the hoss into your
corral. You'll find him there in the morning, and no
one will know but that he got lost and joined the other
horses."

Then she burst out. "But you—*you*—what will become of you? You'll be ketched!"

"I'll manage to get away," he said in a low voice,
"ef—ef"—

"Ef what?" she said tremblingly.

"Ef you'll put the heart in me again,—as you did!" he gasped.

She tried to laugh—to move away. She could do neither. Suddenly he caught her in his arms, with a long kiss, which she returned again and again. Then they stood embraced as they had embraced two days before, but no longer the same. For the cool, lazy Salomy Jane had been transformed into another woman —a passionate, clinging savage. Perhaps something of her father's blood had surged within her at that supreme moment. The man stood erect and determined.

"Wot's your name?" she whispered quickly. It was a woman's quickest way of defining her feelings.

"Dart."

"Yer first name?"

"Jack."

"Let me go now, Jack. Lie low in the woods till tomorrow sunup. I'll come again."

He released her. Yet she lingered a moment. "Put on those things," she said, with a sudden happy flash of eyes and teeth, "and lie close till I come." And then she sped away home.

But midway up the distance she felt her feet going slower, and something at her heartstrings seemed to be pulling her back. She stopped, turned, and glanced to where he had been standing. Had she seen him then, she might have returned. But he had disappeared. She gave her first sigh, and then ran quickly again. It must be nearly ten o'clock! It was not very long to morning!

She was within a few steps of her own door, when the sleeping woods and silent air appeared to suddenly awake with a sharp "crack!"

She stopped, paralyzed. Another "crack!" followed, that echoed over to the far corral. She recalled herself instantly and dashed off wildly to the woods again.

As she ran she thought of one thing only. He had been "dogged" by one of his old pursuers and attacked. But there were two shots, and he was unarmed. Suddenly she remembered that she had left her father's gun standing against the tree where they were talking. Thank God! she may again have saved him. She ran to the tree; the gun was gone. She ran hither and thither, dreading at every step to fall upon his lifeless body. A new thought struck her; she ran to the corral. The horse was not there! He must have been able to regain it, and escaped, *after* the shots had been fired. She drew a long breath of relief, but it was caught up in an apprehension of alarm. Her father, awakened from his sleep by the shots, was hurriedly approaching her.

"What's up now, Salomy Jane?" he demanded excitedly.

"Nothin'," said the girl, with an effort. "Nothin', at least, that *I* can find." She was usually truthful because fearless, and a lie stuck in her throat; but she was no longer fearless, thinking of *him*. "I wasn't abed; so I ran out as soon as I heard the shots fired," she answered in return to his curious gaze.

"And you've hid my gun somewhere where it can't be found," he said reproachfully. "Ef it was that sneak Larrabee, and he fired them shots to lure me out, he might have potted me, without a show, a dozen times in the last five minutes."

She had not thought since of her father's enemy! It

might indeed have been he who had attacked Jack. But she made a quick point of the suggestion. "Run in, Dad, run in and find the gun; you've got no show out here without it." She seized him by the shoulders from behind, shielding him from the woods, and hurried him, half expostulating, half struggling, to the house.

But there no gun was to be found. It was strange; it must have been mislaid in some corner! Was he sure he had not left it in the barn? But no matter now. The danger was over; the Larrabee trick had failed; he must go to bed now, and in the morning they would make a search together. At the same time she had inwardly resolved to rise before him and make another search of the wood, and perhaps—fearful joy as she recalled her promise!—find Jack alive and well, awaiting her!

Salomy Jane slept little that night, nor did her father. But towards morning he fell into a tired man's slumber until the sun was well up the horizon. Far different was it with his daughter: she lay with her face to the window, her head half lifted to catch every sound, from the creaking of the sun-warped shingles above her head to the far-off moan of the rising wind in the pine-trees. Sometimes she fell into a breathless, half-ecstatic trance, living over every moment of the stolen interview; feeling the fugitive's arm still around her, his kisses on her lips; hearing his whispered voice in her ears—the birth of her new life! This was followed again by a period of agonizing dread—that he might even then be lying, his life ebbing away, in the woods, with her name on his lips, and she resting here inactive, until she half started from her bed to go to his succor. And this went on until a pale opal glow

came into the sky, followed by a still paler pink on
the summit of the white Sierras, when she rose and
hurriedly began to dress. Still so sanguine was her
hope of meeting him, that she lingered yet a moment
to select the brown holland skirt and yellow sunbonnet
she had worn when she first saw him. And she had
only seen him twice! Only *twice!* It would be cruel,
too cruel, not to see him again!

She crept softly down the stairs, listening to the long-
drawn breathing of her father in his bedroom, and
then, by the light of a guttering candle, scrawled a
note to him, begging him not to trust himself out of the
house until she returned from her search, and leaving
the note open on the table, swiftly ran out into the
growing day.

Three hours afterwards Mr. Madison Clay awoke to
the sound of loud knocking. At first this forced itself
upon his consciousness as his daughter's regular morning summons, and was responded to by a grunt of
recognition and a nestling closer in the blankets. Then
he awoke with a start and a muttered oath, remember-
ing the events of last night, and his intention to get
up early, and rolled out of bed. Becoming aware by
this time that the knocking was at the outer door, and
hearing the shout of a familiar voice, he hastily pulled
on his boots, his jean trousers, and fastening a single suspender over his shoulder as he clattered down-
stairs, stood in the lower room. The door was open,
and waiting upon the threshold was his kinsman, an
old ally in many a blood-feud—Breckenridge Clay!

"You *are* a cool one, Mad!" said the latter in half-
admiring indignation.

"What's up?" said the bewildered Madison.

"*You* ought to be, and scootin' out o' this," said Breckenridge grimly. "It's all very well to 'know nothin';' but here Phil Larrabee's friends hev just picked him up, drilled through with slugs and deader nor a crow, and now they're lettin' loose Larrabee's two half-brothers on you. And you must go like a derned fool and leave these yer things behind you in the bresh," he went on querulously, lifting Madison Clay's dust-coat, hat, and shotgun from his horse, which stood saddled at the door. "Luckily I picked them up in the woods comin' here. Ye ain't got more than time to get over the state line and among your folks thar afore they'll be down on you. Hustle, old man! What are you gawkin' and starin' at?"

Madison Clay had stared amazed and bewildered —horror-stricken. The incidents of the past night for the first time flashed upon him clearly—hopelessly! The shots; his finding Salomy Jane alone in the woods; her confusion and anxiety to rid herself of him; the disappearance of the shutgun; and now this new discovery of the taking of his hat and coat for a disguise! *She* had killed Phil Larrabee in that disguise, after provoking his first harmless shot! She, his own child, Salomy Jane, had disgraced herself by a man's crime; had disgraced him by usurping his right, and taking a mean advantage, by deceit, of a foe!

"Gimme that gun," he said hoarsely.

Breckenridge handed him the gun in wonder and slowly gathering suspicion. Madison examined nipple and muzzle; one barrel had been discharged. It was true! The gun dropped from his hand.

"Look here, old man," said Breckenridge, with a darkening face, "there's bin no foul play here. Thar's bin no hiring of men, no deputy to do this job. *You* did it fair and square—yourself?"

"Yes, by God!" burst out Madison Clay, in a hoarse voice. "Who says I didn't?"

Reassured, yet believing that Madison Clay had nerved himself for the act by an over-draught of whiskey, which had affected his memory, Breckenridge said curtly, "Then wake up and 'lite' out, ef ye want me to stand by you."

"Go to the corral and pick me out a hoss," said Madison slowly, yet not without a certain dignity of manner. "I've suthin' to say to Salomy Jane afore I go." He was holding her scribbled note, which he had just discovered, in his shaking hand.

Struck by his kinsman's manner, and knowing the dependent relations of father and daughter, Breckenridge nodded and hurried away. Left to himself, Madison Clay ran his fingers through his hair, and straightened out the paper on which Salomy Jane had scrawled her note, turned it over, and wrote on the back:—

You might have told me you did it, and not leave your ole father to find it out how you disgraced yourself with him, too, by a low-down, underhanded, woman's trick! I've said I done it, and took the blame myself, and all the sneakiness of it that folks suspect. If I get away alive—and I don't care much which—you needn't foller. The house and stock are yours; but you ain't any longer the daughter of your disgraced father,

MADISON CLAY.

He had scarcely finished the note when, with a

clatter of hoofs and a led horse, Breckenridge reappeared at the door elate and triumphant. "You're in nigger luck, Mad! I found that stole hoss of Judge Boompointer's had got away and strayed among your stock in the corral. Take him and you're safe; he can't be outrun this side of the state line."

"I ain't no hoss-thief," said Madison grimly.

"Nobody sez ye are, but you'd be wuss—a fool—ef you didn't take him. I'm testimony that you found him among your hosses; I'll tell Judge Boompointer you've got him, and ye kin send him back when you're safe. The judge will be mighty glad to get him back, and call it quits. So ef you've writ to Salomy Jane, come."

Madison Clay no longer hesitated. Salomy Jane might return at any moment,—it would be part of her "fool womanishness,"—and he was in no mood to see her before a third party. He laid the note on the table, gave a hurried glance around the house, which he grimly believed he was leaving forever, and, striding to the door, leaped on the stolen horse, and swept away with his kinsman.

But that note lay for a week undisturbed on the table in full view of the open door. The house was invaded by leaves, pine cones, birds, and squirrels during the hot, silent, empty days, and at night by shy, stealthy creatures, but never again, day or night, by any of the Clay family. It was known in the district that Clay had flown across the state line, his daughter was believed to have joined him the next day, and the house was supposed to be locked up. It lay off the main road, and few passed that way. The starving cattle in the corral at last broke bounds and spread over the woods. And one night a stronger blast than usual swept through the house and carried the note from the table to the floor, where, whirled into a crack in the flooring, it slowly rotted.

But though the sting of her father's reproach was spared her, Salomy Jane had no need of the letter to know what had happened. For as she entered the woods in the dim light of that morning, she saw the figure of Dart gliding from the shadow of a pine towards her. The unaffected cry of joy that rose from her lips died there as she caught sight of his face in the open light.

"You are hurt," she said, clutching his arm passionately.

"No," he said. "But I wouldn't mind that if"—

"You're thinkin' I was afeard to come back last night when I heard the shootin', but I *did* come," she went on feverishly. "I ran back here when I heard the two shots, but you were gone. I went to the corral, but your hoss wasn't there, and I thought you'd got away."

"I *did* get away," said Dart gloomily. "I killed the man, thinkin' he was huntin' *me,* and forgettin' I was disguised. He thought I was your father."

"Yes," said the girl joyfully, "he was after dad, and *you*—you killed him." She again caught his hand admiringly.

But he did not respond. Possibly there were points of honor which this horse-thief felt vaguely with her father. "Listen," he said grimly. "Others think it was your father killed him. When *I* did it—for he fired at me first—I ran to the corral again and took my hoss, thinkin' I might be follered. I made a clear circuit of the house, and when I found he was the only one, and no one was follerin', I come back here and took off my disguise. Then I heard his friends find him in the wood, and I know they suspected your father. And then another man come through the woods while I was hidin' and found the clothes and took them away." He stopped and stared at her gloomily.

But all this was unintelligible to the girl. "Dad would have got the better of him ef you hadn't," she said eagerly, "so what's the difference?"

"All the same," he said gloomily, "I must take his place."

She did not understand, but turned her head to her master. "Then you'll go back with me and tell him *all?*" she said obediently.

"Yes," he said.

She put her hand in his, and they crept out of the wood together. She foresaw a thousand difficulties, but, chiefest of all, that he did not love as she did. *She* would not have taken these risks against their happiness.

But alas for ethics and heroism. As they were issuing from the wood they heard the sound of galloping hoofs, and had barely time to hide themselves before Madison Clay, on the stolen horse of Judge Boompointer, swept past them with his kinsman.

Salomy Jane turned to her lover.

And here I might, as a moral romancer, pause, leaving the guilty, passionate girl eloped with her disreputable lover, destined to lifelong shame and misery, misunderstood to the last by a criminal, fastidious parent. But I am confronted by certain facts, on which this romance is based. A month later a handbill was posted on one of the sentinel pines, announcing that the property would be sold by auction to the highest bidder by Mrs. John Dart, daughter of Madison Clay, Esq., and it was sold accordingly. Still later—by ten years—the chronicler of these pages visited a certain "stock" or "breeding farm," in the "Blue Grass Country," famous for the popular racers it has produced. He was told that the owner was the "best judge of horseflesh in the country." "Small wonder," added his informant, "for they say as a young man out in California he was a horse-thief, and only saved himself by eloping with some rich farmer's daughter. But he's a straight-out and respectable man now, whose word about horses can't be bought; and as for his wife, *she's* a beauty! To see her at the 'Springs,' rigged out in the latest fashion, you'd never think she had ever lived out of New York or wasn't the wife of one of its millionaires."

THE POET OF SIERRA FLAT

As the enterprising editor of the "Sierra Flat Record" stood at his case setting type for his next week's paper, he could not help hearing the woodpeckers who were busy on the roof above his head. It occurred to him that possibly the birds had not yet learned to recognize in the rude structure any improvement on Nature, and this idea pleased him so much that he incorporated it in the editorial article which he was then doubly composing. For the editor was also printer of the "Record"; and although that remarkable journal was reputed to exert a power felt through all Calaveras and a great part of Tuolumne County, strict economy was one of the conditions of its beneficent existence.

Thus preoccupied, he was startled by the sudden irruption of a small roll of manuscript, which was thrown through the open door and fell at his feet. He walked quickly to the threshold and looked down the tangled trail which led to the highroad. But there was nothing to suggest the presence of his mysterious contributor. A hare limped slowly away, a green-and-gold lizard paused upon a pine stump, the woodpeckers ceased their work. So complete had been his sylvan seclusion, that he found it difficult to connect any human agency with the act; rather the hare seemed to have an inexpressibly guilty look, the woodpeckers to maintain a significant silence, and the lizard to be conscience-stricken into stone.

An examination of the manuscript, however, corrected this injustice to defenseless Nature. It was evidently of human origin,—being verse, and of exceeding bad quality. The editor laid it aside. As he did so he thought he saw a face at the window. Sallying out in some indignation, he penetrated the surrounding thicket in every direction, but his search was as fruitless as before. The poet, if it were he, was gone.

A few days after this the editorial seclusion was invaded by voices of alternate expostulation and entreaty. Stepping to the door, the editor was amazed at beholding Mr. Morgan McCorkle, a well-known citizen of Angel's and a subscriber to the "Record," in the act of urging, partly by force and partly by argument, an awkward young man toward the building. When he had finally effected his object, and, as it were, safely landed his prize in a chair, Mr. McCorkle took off his hat, carefully wiped the narrow isthmus of forehead which divided his black brows from his stubby hair, and, with an explanatory wave of his hand toward his reluctant companion, said, "A borned poet, and the cussedest fool you ever seed!"

Accepting the editor's smile as a recognition of the introduction, Mr. McCorkle panted and went on: "Didn't want to come! 'Mister Editor don't want to see me, Morg,' sez he. 'Milt,' sez I, 'he do; a borned poet like you and a gifted genius like he oughter come

together sociable!' And I fetched him. Ah, will yer?"
The born poet had, after exhibiting signs of great dis-
tress, started to run. But Mr. McCorkle was down
upon him instantly, seizing him by his long linen coat,
and settled him back in his chair. " 'T ain't no use
stampeding. Yer ye are and yer ye stays. For yer a
borned poet,—ef ye are as shy as a jackass rabbit.
Look it 'im now!"

He certainly was not an attractive picture. There
was hardly a notable feature in his weak face, except
his eyes, which were moist and shy, and not unlike
the animal to which Mr. McCorkle had compared
him. It was the face that the editor had seen at the
window.

"Knowed him for fower year,—since he war a boy,"
continued Mr. McCorkle in a loud whisper. "Allers
the same, bless you! Can jerk a rhyme as easy as
turnin' jack. Never had any eddication; lived out in
Missooray all his life. But he's chock full o' poetry.
On'y this mornin' sez I to him,—he camps along o'
me,—'Milt!' sez I, 'are breakfast ready?' and he up
and answers back quite peart and chipper, 'The breakfast it is ready, and the birds is singing free, and it's
risin' in the dawnin' light is happiness to me!' When a
man," said Mr. McCorkle, dropping his voice with
deep solemnity, "gets off things like them, without any
call to do it, and handlin' flapjacks over a cookstove
at the same time,—that man's a borned poet."

There was an awkward pause. Mr. McCorkle
beamed patronizingly on his protégé. The born poet
looked as if he were meditating another flight,—not a
metaphorical one. The editor asked if he could do
anything for them.

"In course you can," responded Mr. McCorkle, "that's jest it. Milt, where's that poetry?"

The editor's countenance fell as the poet produced from his pocket a roll of manuscript. He, however, took it mechanically and glanced over it. It was evidently a duplicate of the former mysterious contribution.

The editor then spoke briefly but earnestly. I regret that I cannot recall his exact words, but it appeared that never before, in the history of the "Record," had the pressure been so great upon its columns. Matters of paramount importance, deeply affecting the material progress of Sierra, questions touching the absolute integrity of Calaveras and Tuolumne as social communities, were even now waiting expression. Weeks, nay, months, must elapse before that pressure would be removed, and the "Record" could grapple with any but the sternest of topics. Again, the editor had noticed with pain the absolute decline of poetry in the foothills of the Sierras. Even the works of Byron and Moore attracted no attention in Dutch Flat, and a prejudice seemed to exist against Tennyson in Grass Valley. But the, editor was not without hope for the future. In the course of four or five years, when the country was settled—

"What would be the cost to print this yer?" interrupted Mr. McCorkle quietly.

"About fifty dollars, as an advertisement," responded the editor with cheerful alacrity.

Mr. McCorkle placed the sum in the editor's hand. "Yer see thet's what I sez to Milt. 'Milt,' sez I, 'pay as you go, for you are a borned poet. Hevin' no call to write, but doin' it free and spontaneous like, in course you pays. Thet's why Mr. Editor never printed your poetry.' "

"What name shall I put to it?" asked the editor.

"Milton."

It was the first word that the born poet had spoken during the interview, and his voice was so very sweet and musical that the editor looked at him curiously, and wondered if he had a sister.

"Milton! Is that all?"

"Thet's his furst name," exclaimed Mr. McCorkle.

The editor here suggested that as there had been another poet of that name—

"Milt might be took for him! Thet's bad," reflected Mr. McCorkle with simple gravity. "Well, put down his full name,—Milton Chubbuck."

The editor made a note of the fact. "I'll set it up now," he said. This was also a hint that the interview was ended. The poet and patron, arm in arm, drew towards the door. "In next week's paper," said the editor smilingly, in answer to the child-like look of inquiry in the eyes of the poet, and in another moment they were gone.

The editor was as good as his word. He straightway betook himself to his case, and, unrolling the manuscript, began his task. The woodpeckers on the roof recommenced theirs, and in a few moments the former sylvan seclusion was restored. There was no sound in the barren, barn-like room but the birds above, and below the click of the composing-rule as the editor marshaled the types into lines in his stick, and arrayed them in solid columns on the galley. Whatever might have been his opinion of the copy before him, there was no indication of it in his face, which wore the stolid indifference of his craft. Perhaps this was unfortunate, for as the day wore on and the level rays of the sun began to pierce the adjacent thicket, they sought out and discovered an anxious ambush figure drawn up beside the editor's window,— a figure that had sat there motionless for hours. Within, the editor worked on as steadily and impassively as Fate. And without, the born poet of Sierra Flat sat and watched him as waiting its decree.

The effect of the poem on Sierra Flat was remarkable and unprecedented. The absolute vileness of its doggerel, the gratuitous imbecility of its thought, and above all the crowning audacity of the fact that it was the work of a citizen and published in the county paper, brought it instantly into popularity. For many months Calaveras had languished for a sensation; since the last Vigilance Committee nothing had transpired to dispel the listless ennui begotten of stagnant business and growing civilization. In more prosperous moments the office of the "Record" would have been simply gutted and the editor deported; at present the paper was in such demand that the edition was speedily exhausted. In brief, the poem of Mr. Milton Chubbuck came like a special providence to Sierra Flat. It was read by camp-fires, in lonely cabins, in flaring barrooms and noisy saloons, and declaimed from the boxes of stage-coaches. It was sung in Poker Flat with the addition of a local chorus, and danced as an unhallowed rhythmic dance by the Pyrrhic phalanx of One Horse Gulch, known as "The Festive Stags of Calaveras." Some unhappy ambiguities of expression gave rise to many new readings, notes, and commentaries, which, I regret to state, were more often marked by ingenuity, than delicacy of thought or expression.

Never before did poet acquire such sudden local reputation. From the seclusion of McCorkle's cabin and the obscurity of culinary labors he was haled forth into the glowing sunshine of Fame. The name of Chubbuck was written in letters of chalk on unpainted walls and carved with a pick on the sides of tunnels. A drink known variously as "The Chubbuck Tranquilizer" or "The Chubbuck Exalter" was dispensed at the bars. For some weeks a rude design for a Chubbuck statue, made up of illustrations from circus and melodeon posters, representing the genius of Calaveras in brief skirts on a flying steed in the act of crowning the poet Chubbuck, was visible at Keeler's Ferry. The poet himself was overborne with invitations to drink and extravagant congratulations. The meeting between Colonel Starbottle of Siskiyou and Chubbuck, as previously arranged by our "Boston," late of Roaring Camp, is said to have been indescribably affecting. The Colonel embraced him unsteadily. "I could not return to my constituents at Siskiyou, sir, if this hand, which has grasped that of the gifted Prentice and the lamented Poe, should not have been honored by the touch of the godlike Chubbuck. Gentlemen, American literature is looking up. Thank you! I will take sugar in mine." It was "Boston" who indited letters of congratulations from H. W. Longfellow, Tennyson, and Browning to Mr. Chubbuck, deposited them in the Sierra Flat post-office, and obligingly consented to dictate the replies.

The simple faith and unaffected delight with which these manifestations were received by the poet and his patron might have touched the hearts of these grim masters of irony, but for the sudden and equal development in both of the variety of weak natures. Mr. McCorkle basked in the popularity of his protégé, and became alternately supercilious or patronizing toward the dwellers of Sierra Flat; while the poet, with hair carefully oiled and curled, and bedecked with cheap jewelry and flaunting neck-handkerchief, paraded himself before the single hotel. As may be imagined, this new disclosure of weakness afforded intense satisfaction to Sierra Flat, gave another lease of popularity to the poet, and suggested another idea to the facetious "Boston."

At that time a young lady popularly and professionally known as the "California Pet" was performing to enthusiastic audiences in the interior. Her specialty lay in the personation of youthful masculine character; as a *gamin* of the street she was irresistible, as a Negro-dancer she carried the honest miner's heart by storm. A saucy, pretty brunette, she had preserved a wonderful moral reputation even under the Jove-like advances of showers of gold that greeted her appearance on the stage at Sierra Flat. A prominent and delighted member of that audience was Milton Chubbuck. He attended every night. Every day he lingered at the door of the Union Hotel for a glimpse of the "California Pet." It was not long before he received a note from her,—in "Boston's" most popular and approved female hand,—acknowledging his admiration. It was not long before "Boston" was called upon to indite a suitable reply. At last, in furtherance of his facetious design, it became necessary for "Boston" to call upon the young actress herself and secure her personal participation. To her he unfolded a plan, the successful carrying out of which he felt would secure his fame to posterity as a practical humorist. The "California Pet's" black eyes sparkled approvingly and mischievously. She only stipulated that she should see the man first,—a concession to her feminine weakness which years of dancing Juba and wearing trousers and boots had not wholly eradicated from her willful breast. By all means, it should be done. And the interview was arranged for the next week.

It must not be supposed that during this interval of popularity Mr. Chubbuck had been unmindful of his poetic qualities. A certain portion of each day he was absent from town,—"a-communin' with natur'," as Mr. McCorkle expressed it,—and actually wandering in the mountain trails, or lying on his back under the trees, or gathering fragrant herbs and the bright-colored berries of the Manzanita. These and his company he generally brought to the editor's office late in the afternoon, often to that enterprising journalist's infinite weariness. Quiet and uncommunicative, he would sit there patiently watching him at his work until the hour for closing the office arrived, when he would as quietly depart. There was something so humble and unobtrusive in these visits, that the editor could not find it in his heart to deny them, and accepting them, like the woodpeckers, as a part of his sylvan surroundings, often forgot even his presence. Once or twice, moved by some beauty of expression in the moist, shy eyes, he felt like seriously admonishing his visitor of his idle folly; but his glance falling upon the oiled hair and the gorgeous necktie he invariably thought better of it. The case was evidently hopeless.

The interview between Mr. Chubbuck and the "California Pet" took place in a private room of the Union Hotel; propriety being respected by the presence of that arch-humorist, "Boston." To this gentleman we are indebted for the only true account of the meeting. However reticent Mr. Chubbuck might have been in the presence of his own sex, toward the fairer portion of humanity he was, like most poets, exceedingly voluble. Accustomed as the "California Pet" had been to excessive compliment, she was fairly embarrassed by the extravagant praises of her visitor. Her personation of boy characters, her dancing of the "champion jig," were particularly dwelt upon with fervid but unmistakable admiration. At last, recovering her audacity and emboldened by the presence of "Boston," the "California Pet" electrified her hearers by demanding, half jestingly, half viciously, if it were as a boy or a girl that she was the subject of his flattering admiration.

"That knocked him out o' time," said the delighted "Boston," in his subsequent account of the interview. "But do you believe the d—d fool actually asked her to take him with her; wanted to engage in the company."

The plan, as briefly unfolded by "Boston," was to prevail upon Mr. Chubbuck to make his appearance in costume (already designed and prepared by the inventor) before a Sierra Flat audience, and recite an original poem at the Hall immediately on the conclusion of the "California Pet's" performance. At a given signal the audience were to rise and deliver a volley of unsavory articles (previously provided by the originator of the scheme); then a select few were to rush on the stage, seize the poet, and, after marching him in triumphal procession through the town, were to deposit him beyond its uttermost limits, with strict injunctions never to enter it again. To the first part of the plan the poet was committed; for the latter portion it was easy enough to find participants.

The eventful night came, and with it an audience that packed the long narrow room with one dense mass of human beings. The "California Pet" never had been so joyous, so reckless, so fascinating and audacious before. But the applause was tame and weak compared to the ironical outburst that greeted the second rising of the curtain and the entrance of the born poet of Sierra Flat. Then there was a hush of expectancy, and the poet stepped to the footlights and stood with his manuscript in his hand.

His face was deadly pale. Either there was some suggestion of his fate in the faces of his audience, or some mysterious instinct told him of his danger. He attempted to speak, but faltered, tottered, and staggered to the wings.

Fearful of losing his prey, "Boston" gave the signal and leaped upon the stage. But at the same moment a light figure darted from behind the scenes, and delivering a kick that sent the discomfited humorist back among the musicians, cut a pigeon-wing, executed a double-shuffle, and then advancing to the footlights with that inimitable look, that audacious swagger and utter abandon which had so thrilled and fascinated them a moment before, uttered the characteristic speech, "Wot are you goin' to hit a man fur when he's down, s-a-a-y?"

The look, the drawl, the action, the readiness, and

above all the downright courage of the little woman, had an effect. A roar of sympathetic applause followed the act. "Cut and run while you can," she whispered hurriedly over her one shoulder, without altering the other's attitude of pert and saucy defiance toward the audience. But even as she spoke, the poet tottered and sank fainting upon the stage. Then she threw a despairing whisper behind the scenes, "Ring down the curtain."

There was a slight movement of opposition in the audience, but among them rose the burly shoulders of Yuba Bill, the tall, erect figure of Henry York, of Sandy Bar, and the colorless, determined face of John Oakhurst. The curtain came down.

Behind it knelt the "California Pet" beside the prostrate poet. "Bring me some water. Run for a doctor! Stop!! CLEAR OUT, ALL OF YOU!"

She had unloosed the gaudy cravat and opened the shirt-collar of the insensible figure before her. Then she burst into an hysterical laugh.

"Manuela!"

Her tiring-woman, a Mexican half-breed, came toward her.

"Help me with him to my dressing-room, quick; then stand outside and wait. If anyone questions you, tell them he's gone. Do you hear? HE's gone."

The old woman did as she was bade. In a few moments the audience had departed. Before morning so also had the "California Pet," Manuela, and the poet of Sierra Flat.

But, alas! with them also had departed the fair fame of the "California Pet." Only a few, and these, it is to be feared, of not best moral character them-

selves, still had faith in the stainless honor of their favorite actress. "It was a mighty foolish thing to do, but
it'll all come out right yet." On the other hand, a majority gave her full credit and approbation for her
undoubted pluck and gallantry, but deplored that she
should have thrown it away upon a worthless object.
To elect for a lover the despised and ridiculed vagrant
of Sierra Flat, who had not even the manliness to
stand up in his own defense, was not only evidence of
inherent moral depravity, but was an insult to the
community. Colonel Starbottle saw in it only another
instance of extreme frailty of the sex; he had known
similar cases; and remembered distinctly, sir, how a
well known Philadelphia heiress, one of the finest
women that ever rode in her kerridge, that, gad, sir!
had thrown over a Southern member of Congress to
consort with a d—d nigger. The Colonel had also noticed a singular look in the dog's eye which he did not
entirely fancy. He would not say anything against the
lady, sir, but he had noticed— And here, haply, the
Colonel became so mysterious and darkly confidential
as to be unintelligible and inaudible to the bystanders.

A few days after the disappearance of Mr. Chubbuck a singular report reached Sierra Flat, and it was
noticed that "Boston," who since the failure of his
elaborate joke had been even more depressed in spirits than is habitual with great humorists, suddenly
found that his presence was required in San Francisco.
But as yet nothing but the vaguest surmises were
afloat, and nothing definite was known.

It was a pleasant afternoon when the editor of the
"Sierra Flat Record" looked up from his case and beheld the figure of Mr. Morgan McCorkle standing in

the doorway. There was a distressed look on the face
of that worthy gentleman that at once enlisted the
editor's sympathizing attention. He held an open letter in his hand as he advanced toward the middle of
the room.

"As a man as has allers borne a fair reputation,"
began Mr. McCorkle slowly, "I should like, if so be as
I could, Mister Editor, to make a correction in the columns of your valooable paper."

Mr. Editor begged him to proceed.

"Ye may not disremember that about a month ago
I fetched here what so be as we'll call a young man
whose name might be as it were Milton—Milton Chubbuck."

Mr. Editor remembered perfectly.

"Thet same party I'd knowed better nor fower year,
two on 'em campin' out together. Not that I'd known
him all the time, fur he war shy and strange at spells,
and had odd ways that I took war nat'ral to a borned
poet. Ye may remember that I said he was a borned
poet?"

The editor distinctly did.

"I picked this same party up in St. Jo., taking a fancy
to his face, and kinder calklating he'd runned away
from home; for I'm a married man, Mr. Editor, and
hev children of my own,—and thinkin' belike he was
a borned poet."

"Well," said the editor.

"And as I said before, I should like now to make
a correction in the columns of your valooable paper."

"What correction?" asked the editor.

"I said, ef you remember my words, as how he was
a borned poet."

"Yes."

"From statements in this yer letter it seems as how I war wrong."

"Well?"

"She war a woman."

COLONEL STARBOTTLE
FOR THE PLAINTIFF

It had been a day of triumph for Colonel Starbottle. First, for his personality, as it would have been difficult to separate the Colonel's achievements from his individuality; second, for his oratorical abilities as a sympathetic pleader; and third, for his functions as the leading legal counsel for the Eureka Ditch Company *versus* the State of California. On his strictly legal performances in this issue I prefer not to speak; there were those who denied them, although the jury had accepted them in the face of the ruling of the half-amused, half-cynical Judge himself. For an hour they had laughed with the Colonel, wept with him, been stirred to personal indignation or patriotic exaltation by his passionate and lofty periods,—what else could they do than give him their verdict? If it was alleged by some that the American eagle, Thomas Jefferson, and the Resolutions of '98 had nothing whatever to do with the contest of a ditch company over a doubtfully worded legislative document; that wholesale abuse of the State Attorney and his political motives had not the slightest connection with the legal question raised—it was, nevertheless, generally ac-

121

cepted that the losing party would have been only too glad to have the Colonel on their side. And Colonel Starbottle knew this, as, perspiring, florid, and panting, he rebuttoned the lower buttons of his blue frockcoat, which had become loosed in an oratorical spasm, and readjusted his old-fashioned, spotless shirt frill above it as he strutted from the court-room amidst the hand-shakings and acclamations of his friends.

And here an unprecedented thing occurred. The Colonel absolutely declined spirituous refreshment at the neighboring Palmetto Saloon, and declared his intention of proceeding directly to his office in the adjoining square. Nevertheless, the Colonel quitted the building alone, and apparently unarmed, except for his faithful gold-headed stick, which hung as usual from his forearm. The crowd gazed after him with undisguised admiration of this new evidence of his pluck. It was remembered also that a mysterious note had been handed to him at the conclusion of his speech, —evidently a challenge from the State Attorney. It was quite plain that the Colonel—a practiced duelist —was hastening home to answer it.

But herein they were wrong. The note was in a female hand, and simply requested the Colonel to accord an interview with the writer at the Colonel's office as soon as he left the court. But it was an engagement that the Colonel—as devoted to the fair sex as he was to the "code"—was no less prompt in accepting. He flicked away the dust from his spotless white trousers and varnished boots with his handkerchief, and settled his black cravat under his Byron collar as he neared his office. He was surprised, however, on opening the door of his private office, to find his visitor already there; he was still more startled to find her somewhat past middle age and plainly attired. But the Colonel was brought up in a school of Southern politeness, already antique in the republic, and his bow of courtesy belonged to the epoch of his shirt frill and strapped trousers. No one could have detected his disappointment in his manner, albeit his sentences were short and incomplete. But the Colonel's colloquial speech was apt to be fragmentary incoherencies of his larger oratorical utterances.

"A thousand pardons—for—er—having kept a lady waiting—er! But—er—congratulations of friends —and—er—courtesy due to them—er—interfered with—though perhaps only heightened—by procrastination—the pleasure of—ha!" And the Colonel completed his sentence with a gallant wave of his fat but white and well-kept hand:

"Yes! I came to see you along o' that speech of yours. I was in court. When I heard you gettin' it off on that jury, I says to myself, 'That's the kind o' lawyer *I* want. A man that's flowery and convincin'! Just the man to take up our case.' "

"Ah! It's a matter of business, I see," said the Colonel, inwardly relieved, but externally careless. "And —er—may I ask the nature of the case?"

"Well! it's a breach-o'-promise suit," said the visitor calmly.

If the Colonel had been surprised before, he was now really startled, and with an added horror that required all his politeness to conceal. Breach-of-promise cases were his peculiar aversion. He had always held them to be a kind of litigation which could have been obviated by the prompt killing of the masculine offender—in which case he would have gladly defended the killer. But a suit for damages,—*damages!*—with the reading of love-letters before a hilarious jury and court, was against all his instincts. His chivalry was outraged; his sense of humor was small, and in the course of his career he had lost one or two important cases through an unexpected development of this quality in a jury.

The woman had evidently noticed his hesitation, but mistook its cause. "It ain't me—but my darter."

The Colonel recovered his politeness. "Ah! I am relieved, my dear madam! I could hardly conceive a man ignorant enough to—er—er—throw away such evident good fortune—or base enough to deceive the trustfulness of womanhood—matured and experienced only in the chivalry of our sex, ha!"

The woman smiled grimly. "Yes!—it's my darter, Zaidee Hooker—so ye might spare some of them pretty speeches for *her* before the jury."

The Colonel winced slightly before this doubtful prospect, but smiled. "Ha! Yes!—certainly—the jury. But—er—my dear lady, need we go as far as that? Cannot this affair be settled—er—out of court? Could not this—er—individual—be admonished—told that he must give satisfaction—personal satisfaction—for his dastardly conduct—to—er—near relative—or even valued personal friend? The—er—arrangements necessary for that purpose I myself would undertake."

He was quite sincere; indeed, his small black eyes shone with that fire which a pretty woman or an "affair of honor" could alone kindle. The visitor stared vacantly at him, and said slowly, "And what good is that goin' to do *us?*"

"Compel him to—er—perform his promise," said the Colonel, leaning back in his chair.

"Ketch him doin' it!" she exclaimed scornfully. "No—that ain't wot we're after. We must make him *pay!* Damages—and nothin' short o' *that.*"

The Colonel bit his lip. "I suppose," he said gloomily, "you have documentary evidence—written promises and protestations—er—er—love-letters, in fact?"

"No—nary a letter! Ye see, that's jest it—and that's where *you* come in. You've got to convince that jury yourself. You've got to show what it is—tell the whole story your own way. Lord! to a man like you that's nothin'."

Startling as this admission might have been to any other lawyer, Starbottle was absolutely relieved by it. The absence of any mirth-provoking correspondence, and the appeal solely to his own powers of persuasion, actually struck his fancy. He lightly put aside the compliment with a wave of his white hand.

"Of course," he said confidently, "there is strongly presumptive and corroborative evidence? Perhaps you can give me—er—a brief outline of the affair?"

"Zaidee kin do that straight enough, I reckon," said the woman; "what I want to know first is, kin you take the case?"

The Colonel did not hesitate; his curiosity was piqued. "I certainly can. I have no doubt your daughter will put me in possession of sufficient facts and details—to constitute what we call—er—a brief."

"She kin be brief enough—or long enough—for the matter of that," said the woman, rising. The Colonel accepted this implied witticism with a smile.

"And when may I have the pleasure of seeing her?" he asked politely.

"Well, I reckon as soon as I can trot out and call her. She's just outside, meanderin' in the road—kinder shy, ye know, at first."

She walked to the door. The astounded Colonel nevertheless gallantly accompanied her as she stepped out into the street and called shrilly, "You Zaidee!"

A young girl here apparently detached herself from a tree and the ostentatious perusal of an old election poster, and sauntered down towards the office door. Like her mother, she was plainly dressed; unlike her, she had a pale, rather refined face, with a demure mouth and downcast eyes. This was all the Colonel saw as he bowed profoundly and led the way into his office, for she accepted his salutations without lifting her head. He helped her gallantly to a chair, on which she seated herself sideways, somewhat ceremoniously, with her eyes following the point of her parasol as she traced a pattern on the carpet. A second chair offered to the mother, that lady, however, declined. "I reckon to leave you and Zaidee together to talk it out," she said; turning to her daughter, she added, "Jest you tell him all, Zaidee," and before the Colonel could rise again, disappeared from the room. In spite of his professional experience, Starbottle was for a moment embarrassed. The young girl, however, broke the silence without looking up.

"Adoniram K. Hotchkiss," she began, in a monotonous voice, as if it were a recitation addressed to the public, "first began to take notice of me a year ago. Arter that—off and on"—

"One moment," interrupted the astounded Colonel; "do you mean Hotchkiss the President of the Ditch Company?" He had recognized the name of a prominent citizen—a rigid, ascetic, taciturn, middle-aged man—a deacon—and more than that, the head of the company he had just defended. It seemed inconceivable.

"That's him," she continued, with eyes still fixed on the parasol and without changing her monotonous tone—"off and on ever since. Most of the time at the Free-Will Baptist Church—at morning service, prayer-meetings, and such. And at home—outside—er—in the road."

"Is it this gentleman—Mr. Adoniram K. Hotchkiss who—er—promised marriage?" stammered the Colonel.

"Yes."

The Colonel shifted uneasily in his chair. "Most extraordinary! for—you see—my dear young lady —this becomes—a—er—most delicate affair."

"That's what maw said," returned the young woman simply, yet with the faintest smile playing around her demure lips and downcast cheek.

"I mean," said the Colonel, with a pained yet courteous smile, "that this—er—gentleman—is in fact —er—one of my clients."

"That's what maw said too, and of course your knowing him will make it all the easier for you."

A slight flush crossed the Colonel's cheek as he returned quickly and a little stiffly, "On the contrary— er—it may make it impossible for me to—er—act in this matter."

The girl lifted her eyes. The Colonel held his breath

as the long lashes were raised to his level. Even to an ordinary observer that sudden revelation of her eyes seemed to transform her face with subtle witchery. They were large, brown, and soft, yet filled with an extraordinary penetration and prescience. They were the eyes of an experienced woman of thirty fixed in the face of a child. What else the Colonel saw there Heaven only knows! He felt his inmost secrets plucked from him—his whole soul laid bare—his vanity, belligerency, gallantry—even his mediæval chivalry, penetrated, and yet illuminated, in that single glance. And when the eyelids fell again, he felt that a greater part of himself had been swallowed up in them.

"I beg your pardon," he said hurriedly. "I mean—this matter may be arranged—er—amicably. My interest with—and as you wisely say—my—er—knowledge of my client—er—Mr. Hotchkiss—may effect —a compromise."

"And *damages*," said the young girl, readdressing her parasol, as if she had never looked up.

The Colonel winced. "And—er—undoubtedly *compensation*—if you do not press a fulfillment of the promise. Unless," he said, with an attempted return to his former easy gallantry, which, however, the recollection of her eyes made difficult, "it is a question of—er—the affections."

"Which?" asked this fair client softly.

"If you still love him?" explained the Colonel, actually blushing.

Zaidee again looked up; again taking the Colonel's breath away with eyes that expressed not only the fullest perception of what he had *said*, but of what he thought and had not said, and with an added subtle suggestion of what he might have thought. "That's tellin'," she said, dropping her long lashes again.

The Colonel laughed vacantly. Then feeling himself growing imbecile, he forced an equally weak gravity. "Pardon me—I understand there are no letters; may I know the way in which he formulated his declaration and promises?"

"Hymn-books."

"I beg your pardon," said the mystified lawyer.

"Hymn-books—marked words in them with pencil —and passed 'em on to me," repeated Zaidee. "Like 'love,' 'dear,' 'precious,' 'sweet,' and 'blessed,'" she added, accenting each word with a push of her parasol on the carpet. "Sometimes a whole line outer Tate and Brady—and Solomon's Song, you know, and sich."

"I believe," said the Colonel loftily, "that the—er— phrases of sacred psalmody lend themselves to the language of the affections. But in regard to the distinct promise of marriage—was there—er—no *other* expression?"

"Marriage Service in the prayer-book—lines and words outer that—all marked," Zaidee replied.

The Colonel nodded naturally and approvingly. "Very good. Were others cognizant of this? Were there any witnesses?"

"Of course not," said the girl. "Only me and him. It was generally at church-time—or prayer-meeting. Once, in passing the plate, he slipped one o' them peppermint lozenges with the letters stamped on it 'I love you' for me to take."

The Colonel coughed slightly. "And you have the lozenge?"

"I ate it."

"Ah," said the Colonel. After a pause he added delicately, "But were these attentions—er—confined to—er—sacred precincts? Did he meet you elsewhere?"

"Useter pass our house on the road," returned the girl, dropping into her monotonous recital, "and useter signal."

"Ah, signal?" repeated the Colonel approvingly.

"Yes! He'd say 'Keerow,' and I'd say 'Keeree.' Suthing like a bird, you know."

Indeed, as she lifted her voice in imitation of the call, the Colonel thought it certainly very sweet and birdlike. At least as *she* gave it. With his remembrance of the grim deacon he had doubts as to the melodiousness of *his* utterance. He gravely made her repeat it.

"And after that signal?" he added suggestively.

"He'd pass on."

The Colonel again coughed slightly, and tapped his desk with his penholder.

"Were there any endearments—er—caresses—er —such as taking your hand—er—clasping your waist?" he suggested, with a gallant yet respectful sweep of his white hand and bowing of his head; "er —slight pressure of your fingers in the changes of a dance—I mean," he corrected himself, with an apologetic cough—"in the passing of the plate?"

"No; he was not what you'd call 'fond,' " returned the girl.

"Ah! Adoniram K. Hotchkiss was not 'fond' in the ordinary acceptance of the word," noted the Colonel, with professional gravity.

She lifted her disturbing eyes, and again absorbed

his in her own. She also said "Yes," although her eyes in their mysterious prescience of all he was thinking disclaimed the necessity of any answer at all. He smiled vacantly. There was a long pause; on which she slowly disengaged her parasol from the carpet pattern, and stood up.

"I reckon that's about all," she said.

"Er—yes—but one moment," began the Colonel vaguely. He would have liked to keep her longer, but with her strange premonition of him he felt powerless to detain her, or explain his reason for doing so. He instinctively knew she had told him all; his professional judgment told him that a more hopeless case had never come to his knowledge. Yet he was not daunted, only embarrassed. "No matter," he said. "Of course I shall have to consult with you again."

Her eyes again answered that she expected he would, and she added simply, "When?"

"In the course of a day or two," he replied quickly. "I will send you word."

She turned to go. In his eagerness to open the door for her, he upset his chair, and with some confusion, that was actually youthful, he almost impeded her movements in the hall, and knocked his broad-brimmed Panama hat from his bowing hand in a final gallant sweep. Yet as her small, trim, youthful figure, with its simple Leghorn straw hat confined by a blue bow under her round chin, passed away before him, she looked more like a child than ever.

The Colonel spent that afternoon in making diplomatic inquiries. He found his youthful client was the daughter of a widow who had a small ranch on the crossroads, near the new Free-Will Baptist Church

—the evident theatre of this pastoral. They led a secluded life, the girl being little known in the town, and her beauty and fascination apparently not yet being a recognized fact. The Colonel felt a pleasurable relief at this, and a general satisfaction he could not account for. His few inquiries concerning Mr. Hotchkiss only confirmed his own impressions of the alleged lover,—a serious-minded, practically abstracted man, abstentive of youthful society, and the last man apparently capable of levity of the affections or serious flirtation. The Colonel was mystified, but determined of purpose, whatever that purpose might have been.

The next day he was at his office at the same hour. He was alone—as usual—the Colonel's office being really his private lodgings, disposed in connecting rooms, a single apartment reserved for consultation. He had no clerk, his papers and briefs being taken by his faithful body-servant and ex-slave "Jim" to another firm who did his office work since the death of Major Stryker, the Colonel's only law partner, who fell in a duel some years previous. With a fine constancy the Colonel still retained his partner's name on his doorplate, and, it was alleged by the superstitious, kept a certain invincibility also through the *manes* of that lamented and somewhat feared man.

The Colonel consulted his watch, whose heavy gold case still showed the marks of a providential interference with a bullet destined for its owner, and replaced it with some difficulty and shortness of breath in his fob. At the same moment he heard a step in the passage, and the door opened to Adoniram K. Hotchkiss. The Colonel was impressed; he had a duelist's respect for punctuality.

The man entered with a nod and the expectant in-quiring look of a busy man. As his feet crossed that sacred threshold the Colonel became all courtesy; he placed a chair for his visitor, and took his hat from his half-reluctant hand. He then opened a cupboard and brought out a bottle of whiskey and two glasses.

"A—er—slight refreshment, Mr. Hotchkiss," he suggested politely.

"I never drink," replied Hotchkiss, with the se-vere attitude of a total abstainer.

"Ah—er—not the finest Bourbon whiskey, selected by a Kentucky friend? No? Pardon me! A cigar, then —the mildest Havana."

"I do not use tobacco nor alcohol in any form," re-peated Hotchkiss ascetically. "I have no foolish weak-nesses."

The Colonel's moist, beady eyes swept silently over his client's sallow face. He leaned back comfort-ably in his chair, and half closing his eyes as in dreamy reminiscence, said slowly: "Your reply, Mr. Hotchkiss, reminds me of—er—sing'lar circumstance that—er—occurred, in point of fact—at the St. Charles Hotel, New Orleans. Pinkey Hornblower— personal friend—invited Senator Doolittle to join him in social glass. Received, sing'larly enough, reply simi-lar to yours. 'Don't drink nor smoke?' said Pinkey. 'Gad, sir, you must be mighty sweet on the ladies.' Ha!" The Colonel paused long enough to allow the faint flush to pass from Hotchkiss's cheek, and went on, half closing his eyes: " 'I allow no man, sir, to dis-cuss my personal habits,' declared Doolittle, over his shirt collar. 'Then I reckon shootin' must be one of those habits,' said Pinkey coolly. Both men drove out on the Shell Road back of cemetery next morning. Pinkey put bullet at twelve paces through Doolittle's temple. Poor Doo never spoke again. Left three wives and seven children, they say—two of 'em black."

"I got a note from you this morning," said Hotchkiss, with badly concealed impatience. "I suppose in reference to our case. You have taken judgment, I believe."

The Colonel, without replying, slowly filled a glass of whiskey and water. For a moment he held it dreamily before him, as if still engaged in gentle reminiscences called up by the act. Then tossing it off, he wiped his lips with a large white handkerchief, and leaning back comfortably in his chair, said, with a wave of his hand, "The interview I requested, Mr. Hotchkiss, concerns a subject—which I may say is— er—er—at present *not* of a public or business nature —although *later* it might become—er—er—both. It is an affair of some—er—delicacy."

The Colonel paused, and Mr. Hotchkiss regarded him with increased impatience. The Colonel, however, continued, with unchanted deliberation: "It concerns—er—er—a young lady—a beautiful, high-souled creature, sir, who, apart from her personal loveliness—er—er—I may say is of one of the first families of Missouri, and—er—not remotely connected by marriage with one of—er—er—my boyhood's dearest friends." The latter, I grieve to say, was a pure invention of the Colonel's—an oratorical addition to the scanty information he had obtained the previous day. "The young lady," he continued blandly, "enjoys the further distinction of being the object of such attention from you as would make this interview—really—a confidential matter—er—er—among friends and—er—er—relations in present and future. I need not say that the lady I refer to is Miss Zaidee Juno Hooker, only daughter of Almira Ann Hooker, relict of Jefferson Brown Hooker, formerly of Bone County, Kentucky, and latterly of—er—Pike County, Missouri."

The sallow, ascetic hue of Mr. Hotchkiss's face had passed through a livid and then a greenish shade, and finally settled into a sullen red. "What's all this about?" he demanded roughly.

The least touch of belligerent fire came into Starbottle's eye, but his bland courtesy did not change. "I believe," he said politely, "I have made myself clear as between—er—gentlemen, though perhaps not as clear as I should to—er—er—jury."

Mr. Hotchkiss was apparently stuck with some significance in the lawyer's reply. "I don't know," he said, in a lower and more cautious voice, "what you mean by what you call 'my attentions' to—anyone—or how it concerns you. I have not exchanged half a dozen words with—the person you name—have never written her a line—nor even called at her house.

He rose with an assumption of ease, pulled down his waistcoat, buttoned his coat, and took up his hat. The Colonel did not move.

"I believe I have already indicated my meaning in what I have called 'your attentions,' " said the Colonel blandly, "and given you my 'concern' for speaking as—er—er—mutal friend. As to your statement of your relations with Miss Hooker, I may state that it is fully corroborated by the statement of the young lady herself in this very office yesterday."

"Then what does this impertinent nonsense mean? Why am I summoned here?" demanded Hotchkiss furiously.

"Because," said the Colonel deliberately, "that statement is infamously—yes, damnably to your discredit, sir!"

Mr. Hotchkiss was here seized by one of those impotent and inconsistent rages which occasionally betray the habitually cautious and timid man. He caught up the Colonel's stick, which was lying on the table. At the same moment the Colonel, without any apparent effort, grasped it by the handle. To Mr. Hotchkiss's astonishment, the stick separated in two pieces, leaving the handle and about two feet of narrow glitering steel in the Colonel's hand. The man recoiled, dropping the useless fragment. The Colonel picked it up, fitted the shining blade in it, clicked the spring, and then rising with a face of courtesy yet of unmistakeably genuine pain, and with even a slight tremor in his voice, said gravely,—

"Mr. Hotchkiss, I owe you a thousand apologies, sir, that—er—a weapon should be drawn by me— even through your own inadvertence—under the sacred protection of my roof, and upon an unarmed man. I beg your pardon, sir, and I even withdraw the expressions which provoked that inadvertence. Nor does this apology prevent you from holding me responsible—personally reponsible *elsewhere* for an indiscretion committed in behalf of a lady—my—er— client."

"Your client? Do you mean you have taken her case? You, the counsel for the Ditch Company?" asked Mr. Hotchkiss, in trembling indignation.

"Having won *your* case, sir," replied the Colonel coolly, "the—er—usages of advocacy do not prevent me from espousing the cause of the weak and unprotected."

"We shall see, sir," said Hotchkiss, grasping the handle of the door and backing into the passage. "There are other lawyers who"—

"Permit me to see you out," interrupted the Colonel, rising politely.

—"will be ready to resist the attacks of blackmail," continued Hotchkiss, retreating along the passage.

"And then you will be able to repeat your remarks to me *in the street*," continued the Colonel, bowing, as he persisted in following his visitor to the door.

But here Mr. Hotchkiss quickly slammed it behind him, and hurried away. The Colonel returned to his office, and sitting down, took a sheet of letter-paper bearing the inscription "Starbottle and Stryker, Attorneys and Counselors," and wrote the following lines:—

HOOKER *versus* HOTCHKISS.

DEAR MADAM,—Having had a visit from the defendant in above, we should be pleased to have an interview with you at two P. M. to-morrow.

Your obedient servants,
STARBOTTLE AND STRYKER.

This he sealed and dispatched by his trusted servant Jim, and then devoted a few moments to reflection. It was the custom of the Colonel to act first, and justify the action by reason afterwards.

He knew that Hotchkiss would at once lay the mat-

ter before rival counsel. He knew that they would
advise him that Miss Hooker had "no case"—that
she would be non-suited on her own evidence, and he
ought not to compromise, but be ready to stand trial.
He believed, however, that Hotchkiss feared such exposure, and although his own instincts had been at
first against this remedy, he was now instinctively in
favor of it. He remembered his own power with a jury;
his vanity and his chivalry alike approved of this
heroic method; he was bound by no prosaic facts—
he had his own theory of the case, which no mere evidence could gainsay. In fact, Mrs. Hooker's admission that he was to "tell the story in his own way" actually appeared to him an inspiration and a prophecy.

Perhaps there was something else, due possibly to
the lady's wonderful eyes, of which he had thought
much. Yet it was not her simplicity that affected him
solely; on the contrary, it was her apparent intelligent
reading of the character of her recreant lover—and
of his own! Of all the Colonel's previous "light" or
"serious" loves, none had ever before flattered him in
that way. And it was this, combined with the respect
which he had held for their professional relations,
that precluded his having a more familiar knowledge
of his client, through serious questioning or playful
gallantry. I am not sure it was not part of the charm
to have a rustic *femme incomprise* as a client.

Nothing could exceed the respect with which he
greeted her as she entered his office the next day. He
even affected not to notice that she had put on her
best clothes, and, he made no doubt, appeared as
when she had first attracted the mature yet faithless

attentions of Deacon Hotchkiss at church. A white virginal muslin was belted around her slim figure by a blue ribbon, and her Leghorn hat was drawn around her oval cheek by a bow of the same color. She had a Southern girl's narrow feet, encased in white stockings and kid slippers, which were crossed primly before her as she sat in a chair, supporting her arm by her faithful parasol planted firmly on the floor. A faint odor of southernwood exhaled from her, and, oddly enough, stirred the Colonel with a far-off recollection of a pine-shaded Sunday-school on a Georgia hillside, and of his first love, aged ten, in a short starched frock. Possibly it was the same recollection that revived something of the awkwardness he had felt then.

He, however, smiled vaguely, and sitting down, coughed slightly, and placed his finger-tips together. "I have had an—er—interview with Mr. Hotchkiss, but—I—er—regret to say there seems to be no prospect of—er—compromise."

He paused, and to his surprise her listless "company" face lit up with an adorable smile. "Of course! —ketch him!" she said. "Was he mad when you told him?" She put her knees comfortably together and leaned forward for a reply.

For all that, wild horses could not have torn from the Colonel a word about Hotchkiss's anger. "He expressed his intention of employing counsel—and defending a suit," returned the Colonel, affably basking in her smile.

She dragged her chair nearer his desk. "Then you'll fight him tooth and nail?" she asked eagerly;

"you'll show him up? You'll tell the whole story your own way? You'll give him fits?—and you'll make him pay? Sure?" she went on breathlessly.

"I—er—will," said the Colonel almost as breathlessly.

She caught his fat white hand, which was lying on the table, between her own and lifted it to her lips. He felt her soft young fingers even through the isle-thread gloves that encased them, and the warm moisture of her lips upon his skin. He felt himself flushing—but was unable to break the silence or change his posi-tion. The next moment she had scuttled back with her chair to her old position.

"I—er—certainly shall do my best," stammered the Colonel, in an attempt to recover his dignity and composure.

"That's enough! You'll *do* it," said she enthusias-tically. "Lordy! Just you talk for *me* as ye did for *his* old Ditch Company, and you'll fetch it—every time! Why, when you made that jury sit up the other day —when you got that off about the Merrikan flag wav-ing equally over the rights of honest citizens banded together in peaceful commercial pursuits, as well as over the fortress of official proflig—"

"Oligarchy," murmured the Colonel courteously.

—"oligarchy," repeated the girl quickly, "my breath was just took away. I said to maw, 'Ain't he too sweet for anything!' I did, honest Injin! And when you rolled it all off at the end—never missing a word (you didn't need to mark 'em in a lesson-book, but had 'em all ready on your tongue)—and walked out— Well! I didn't know you nor the Ditch Company 'from Adam, but I could have just run over and kissed you there before the whole court!"

She laughed, with her face glowing, although her strange eyes were cast down. Alack! The Colonel's face was equally flushed, and his own beady eyes were on his desk. To any other woman he would have voiced the banal gallantry that he should now, himself, look forward to that reward, but the words never reached his lips. He laughed, coughed slightly, and when he looked up again she had fallen into the same attitude as on her first visit, with her parasol point on the floor.

"I must ask you to—er—direct your memory to—er—another point: the breaking off of the—er—er—er—engagement. Did he—er—give any reason for it? Or show any cause?"

"No; he never said anything," returned the girl.

"Not in his usual way?—er—no reproaches out of the hymnbook?—or the sacred writings?"

"No; he just *quit*."

"Er—ceased his attentions," said the Colonel gravely. "And naturally you—er—were not conscious of any cause for his doing so."

The girl raised her wonderful eyes so suddenly and so penetratingly without replying in any other way that the Colonel could only hurriedly say: "I see! None, of course!"

At which she rose, the Colonel rising also. "We—shall begin proceedings at once. I must, however, caution you to answer no questions, nor say anything about this case to anyone until you are in court."

She answered his request with another intelligent

look and a nod. He accompanied her to the door. As he took her proffered hand, he raised the lisle-thread fingers to his lips with old-fashioned gallantry. As if that act had condoned for his first omissions and awkwardness, he became his old-fashioned self again, buttoned his coat, pulled out his shirt frill, and strutted back to his desk.

A day or two later it was known throughout the town that Zaidee Hooker had sued Adoniram Hotchkiss for breach of promise, and that the damages were laid at five thousand dollars. As in those bucolic days the Western press was under the secure censorship of a revolver, a cautious tone of criticism prevailed, and any gossip was confined to personal expression, and even then at the risk of the gossiper. Nevertheless, the situation provoked the intensest curiosity. The Colonel was approached—until his statement that he should consider any attempt to overcome his professional secrecy a personal reflection withheld further advances. The community were left to the more ostentatious information of the defendant's counsel, Messrs. Kitcham and Bilser, that the case was "ridiculous" and "rotten," that the plaintiff would be nonsuited, and the fire-eating Starbottle would be taught a lesson that he could not "bully" the law, and there were some dark hints of a conspiracy. It was even hinted that the "case" was the revengeful and preposterous outcome of the refusal of Hotchkiss to pay Starbottle an extravagant fee for his late services to the Ditch Company. It is unnecessary to say that these words were not reported to the Colonel. It was, however, an unfortunate circumstance for the calmer, ethical consideration of the subject that the Church sided with Hotchkiss, as this provoked an equal adherence to the plaintiff and Starbottle on the part of the larger body of non-church-goers, who were delighted at a possible exposure of the weakness of religious rectitude. "I've allus had my suspicions o' them early candle-light meetings down at that gospel shop," said one critic, "and I reckon Deacon Hotchkiss didn't rope in the gals to attend jest for psalm-singing." "Then for him to get up and leave the board afore the game's finished and try to sneak out of it," said another,—"I suppose that's what they call *religious*."

It was therefore not remarkable that the court-house three weeks later was crowded with an excited multitude of the curious and sympathizing. The fair plaintiff, with her mother, was early in attendance, and under the Colonel's advice appeared in the same modest garb in which she had first visited his office. This and her downcast, modest demeanor were perhaps at first disappointing to the crowd, who had evidently expected a paragon of loveliness in this Circe of that grim, ascetic defendant, who sat beside his counsel. But presently all eyes were fixed on the Colonel, who certainly made up in *his* appearance any deficiency of his fair client. His portly figure was clothed in a blue dress coat with brass buttons, a buff waistcoat which permitted his frilled shirt-front to become erectible above it, a black satin stock which confined a boyish turned-down collar around his full neck, and immaculate drill trousers, strapped over varnished boots. A murmur ran round the court. "Old 'Personally Responsible' has got his war-point on"; "The Old War-Horse is smelling powder," were whispered comments. Yet for all that, the most irreverent among them recognized vaguely, in this bizarre figure, something of an honored past in their country's history, and possibly felt the spell of old deeds and old names that had once thrilled their boyish pulses. The new District Judge returned Colonel Starbottle's profoundly punctilious bow. The Colonel was followed by his Negro servant, carrying a parcel of hymn-books and Bibles, who, with a courtesy evidently imitated from his master, placed one before the opposite counsel. This, after a first curious glance, the lawyer somewhat superciliously tossed aside. But when Jim, proceeding to the jury-box, placed with equal politeness the remaining copies before the jury, the opposite counsel sprang to his feet.

"I want to direct the attention of the Court to this unprecedented tampering with the jury, by this gratuitous exhibition of matter impertinent and irrelevant to the issue."

The Judge cast an inquiring look at Colonel Starbottle.

"May it please the Court," returned Colonel Starbottle with dignity, ignoring the counsel, "the defendant's counsel will observe that he is already furnished with the matter—which I regret to say he has treated—in the presence of the Court—and of his client, a deacon of the church—with—er—great superciliousness. When I state to Your Honor that the books in question are hymn-books and copies of the Holy Scriptures, and that they are for the instruction of the jury, to whom I shall have to refer them in the course of my opening, I believe I am within my rights."

"The act is certainly unprecedented," said the Judge dryly, "but unless the counsel for the plaintiff expects the jury to *sing* from these hymn-books, their introduction is not improper, and I cannot admit the objection. As defendant's counsel are furnished with copies also, they cannot plead 'surprise,' as in the introduction of new matter, and as plaintiff's counsel relies evidently upon the jury's attention to his opening, he would not be the first person to distract it." After a pause he added, addressing the Colonel, who remained standing, "The Court is with you, sir; proceed."

But the Colonel remained motionless and statuesque, with folded arms.

"I have overruled the objection," repeated the Judge; "you may go on."

"I am waiting, Your Honor, for the—er—withdrawal by the defendant's counsel of the word 'tampering,' as refers to myself, and of 'impertinent,' as refers to the sacred volumes."

"The request is a proper one, and I have no doubt will be acceded to," returned the Judge quietly. The defendant's counsel rose and mumbled a few words of apology, and the incident closed. There was, however, a general feeling that the Colonel had in some way "scored," and if his object had been to excite the greatest curiosity about the books, he had made his point.

But impassive of his victory, he inflated his chest, with his right hand in the breast of his buttoned coat, and began. His usual high color had paled slightly, but the small pupils of his prominent eyes glittered like steel. The young girl leaned forward in her chair with an attention so breathless, a sympathy so quick, and an admiration so artless and unconscious that in an instant she divided with the speaker the attention of the whole assemblage. It was very hot; the court was crowded to suffocation; even the open windows revealed a crowd of faces outside the building, eagerly following the Colonel's words.

He would remind the jury that only a few weeks ago he stood there as the advocate of a powerful Company, then represented by the present defendant. He spoke then as the champion of strict justice against legal oppression; no less should he to-day champion the cause of the unprotected and the comparatively defenseless—save for that paramount power which surrounds beauty and innocence—even though the plaintiff of yesterday was the defendant of to-day. As he approached the court a moment ago he had raised his eyes and beheld the starry flag flying from its dome, and he knew that glorious banner was a symbol of the perfect equality, under the Constitution, of the rich and the poor, the strong and the weak —an equality which made the simple citizen taken from the plough in the field, the pick in the gulch, or from behind the counter in the mining town, who served on that jury, the equal arbiters of justice with that highest legal luminary whom they were proud to welcome on the bench to-day. The Colonel paused, with a stately bow to the impassive Judge. It was this, he continued, which lifted his heart as he approached the building. And yet—he had entered it with an uncertain—he might almost say—a timid step. And why? He knew, gentlemen, he was about to confront a profound—ay! a sacred responsibility! Those hymn-books and holy writings handed to the jury were *not*, as His Honor had surmised, for the purpose of enabling the jury to indulge in—er—preliminary choral exercise! He might, indeed, say, "Alas, not!" They were the damning, incontrovertible proofs of the perfidy of the defendant. And they would prove as terrible a warning to him as the fatal characters upon Belshazzar's wall. There was a strong sensation. Hotchkiss turned a sallow green. His lawyers assumed a careless smile.

It was his duty to tell them that this was not one of those ordinary "breach-of-promise" cases which were too often the occasion of ruthless mirth and indecent levity in the court-room. The jury would find nothing of that here. There were no love-letters with the epithets of endearment, nor those mystic crosses and ciphers which, he had been credibly informed, chastely hid the exchange of those mutual caresses known as "kisses." There was no cruel tearing of the veil from those sacred privacies of the human affection; there was no forensic shouting out of those fond confidences meant only for *one*. But there was, he was shocked to say, a new sacrilegious intrusion. The weak pipings of Cupid were mingled with the chorus of the saints,—the sanctity of the temple known as the "meeting-house" was desecrated by proceedings more in keeping with the shrine of Venus; and the inspired writings themselves were used as the medium of amatory and wanton flirtation by the defendant in his sacred capacity as deacon.

The Colonel artistically paused after this thunderous denunciation. The jury turned eagerly to the leaves of the hymn-books, but the larger gaze of the audience remained fixed upon the speaker and the girl, who sat in rapt admiration of his periods. After the hush, the Colonel continued in a lower and sadder voice: "There are, perhaps, few of us here, gentlemen, —with the exception of the defendant,—who can arrogate to themselves the title of regular church-goers, or to whom these humbler functions of the prayer-meeting, the Sunday-school, and the Bible-class are habitually familiar. Yet"—more solemnly—"down in our hearts is the deep conviction of our shortcomings and failings, and a laudable desire that others, at least, should profit by the teachings we neglect. Perhaps," he continued, closing his eyes dreamily, "there is not a man here who does not recall the happy days of his boyhood, the rustic village spire, the lessons shared with some artless village maiden, with whom he later sauntered, hand in hand, through the woods, as the simple rhyme rose upon their lips—

'Always make it a point to have it a rule,
Never to be late at the Sabbath-school.'

He would recall the strawberry feasts, the welcome annual picnic, redolent with hunks of gingerbread and sarsaparilla. How would they feel to know that these scared recollections were now forever profaned in their memory by the knowledge that the defendant was capable of using such occasions to make love to the larger girls and teachers, whilst his artless companions were innocently—the Court will pardon me for introducing what I am credibly informed is the local expression—'doing gooseberry'?" The tremulous flicker of a smile passed over the faces of the listening crowd, and the Colonel slightly winced. But he recovered himself instantly, and continued,—

"My client, the only daughter of a widowed mother —who has for years stemmed the varying tides of adversity, in the western precincts of this town—stands before you to-day invested only in her own innocence. She wears no—er—rich gifts of her faithless admirer—is panoplied in no jewels, rings, nor mementos of affection such as lovers delight to hang upon the shrine of their affections; hers is not the glory with which Solomon decorated the Queen of Sheba, though the defendant, as I shall show later, clothed her in the less expensive flowers of the king's poetry. No, gentlemen! The defendant exhibited in this affair a certain frugality of—er—percuniary investment, which I am willing to admit may be commendable in his class. His only gift was characteristic alike of his methods and his economy. There is, I understand, a certain not unimportant feature of religious exercise known as 'taking a collection.' The defendant, on this occasion, by the mute presentation of a tin plate covered with baize, solicited the pecuniary contributions of the faithful. On approaching the plaintiff, however, he himself slipped a love-token upon the plate and pushed it towards her. That love-token was a lozenge—a small disk, I have reason to believe, concocted of peppermint and sugar, bearing upon its reverse surface the simple words, 'I love you!' I have since ascertained that these disks may be bought for five cents a dozen —or at considerably less than one half cent for the single lozenge. Yes, gentlemen, the words 'I love you!' —the oldest legend of all; the refrain 'when the morning stars sang together'—were presented to the plaintiff by a medium so insignificant that there is, happily, no coin in the republic low enough to represent its value.

"I shall prove to you, gentlemen of the jury," said the Colonel solemnly, drawing a Bible from his coat-tail pocket, "that the defendant for the last twelve months conducted an amatory correspondence with the plaintiff by means of underlined words of Sacred Writ and church psalmody, such as 'beloved,' 'precious,' and 'dearest,' occasionally appropriating whole passages which seemed apposite to his tender passion. I shall call your attention to one of them. The defendant, while professing to be a total abstainer,—a man who, in my own knowledge, has refused spirituous refreshment as an inordinate weakness of the flesh,—with shameless hypocrisy underscores with his pencil the following passage, and presents it to the plaintiff. The gentlemen of the jury will find it in the Song of Solomon, page 548, chapter ii., verse 5." After a pause, in which the rapid rustling of leaves was heard in the jury-box, Colonel Starbottle declaimed in a pleading, stentorian voice, " 'Stay me with—er—*flagons*, comfort me with—er—apples—for I am—er—sick of love.' Yes, gentlemen!—yes, you may well turn from those accusing pages and look at the double-faced defendant. He desires—to—er—be—'stayed with flagons'! I am not aware at present what kind of liquor is habitually dispensed at these meetings, and for which the defendant so urgently clamored; but it will be my duty, before this trial is over, to discover it, if I have to summon every bar-keeper in this district. For the moment I will simply call your attention to the *quantity*. It is not a single

drink that the defendant asks for—not a glass of light
and generous wine, to be shared with his inamorata,
but a number of flagons or vessels, each possibly holding a pint measure—*for himself!*"

The smile of the audience had become a laugh. The
Judge looked up warningly, when his eye caught the
fact that the Colonel had again winced at this mirth.
He regarded him seriously. Mr. Hotchkiss's counsel
had joined in the laugh affectedly, but Hotchkiss himself sat ashy pale. There was also a commotion in the
jury-box, a hurried turning over of leaves, and an excited discussion.

"The gentlemen of the jury," said the Judge, with
official gravity, "will please keep order and attend
only to the speeches of counsel. Any discussion *here*
is irregular and premature, and must be reserved for
the jury-room after they have retired."

The foreman of the jury struggled to his feet. He
was a powerful man, with a good-humored face, and,
in spite of his unfelicitous nickname of "The Bone-
Breaker," had a kindly, simple but somewhat emo-
tional nature. Nevertheless, it appeared as if he were
laboring under some powerful indignation.

"Can we ask a question, Judge?" he said respectfully, although his voice had the unmistakable Western ring in it, as of one who was unconscious that
he could be addressing any but his peers.

"Yes," said the Judge good-humoredly.

"We're finding in this yere piece, out o' which the
Kernel hes just bin a-quotin', some language that
me and my pardners allow hadn't orter be read out
afore a young lady in court, and we want to know of
you—ez a fa'r-minded and impartial man—ef this is

the reg'lar kind o' book given to gals and babies down at the meetin'-house."

"The jury will please follow the counsel's speech without comment," said the Judge briefly, fully aware that the defendant's counsel would spring to his feet, as he did promptly.

"The Court will allow us to explain to the gentlemen that the language they seem to object to has been accepted by the best theologians for the last thousand years as being purely mystic. As I will explain later, those are merely symbols of the Church"——

"Of wot?" interrupted the foreman, in deep scorn.

"Of the Church!"

"We ain't askin' any questions o' *you*, and we ain't takin' any answers," said the foreman, sitting down abruptly.

"I must insist," said the Judge sternly, "that the plaintiff's counsel be allowed to continue his opening without interruption. You" (to defendant's counsel) "will have your opportunity to reply later."

The counsel sank down in his seat with the bitter conviction that the jury was manifestly against him, and the case as good as lost. But his face was scarcely as disturbed as his client's, who, in great agitation, had begun to argue with him wildly, and was apparently pressing some point against the lawyer's vehement opposal. The Colonel's murky eyes brightened as he still stood erect, with his hand thrust in his breast.

"It will be put to you, gentlemen, when the counsel on the other side refrains from mere interruption and confines himself to reply, that my unfortunate client has no action——no remedy at law——because there

were no spoken words of endearment. But, gentlemen, it will depend upon *you* to say what are and
what are not articulate expressions of love. We all
know that among the lower animals, with whom you
may possibly be called upon to classify the defendant,
there are certain signals more or less harmonious, as
the case may be. The ass brays, the horse neighs, the
sheep bleats—the feathered denizens of the grove call
to their mates in more musical roundelays. These are
recognized facts, gentlemen, which you yourselves,
as dwellers among nature in this beautiful land, are
all cognizant of. They are facts that no one would
deny—and we should have a poor opinion of the ass
who, at—er—such a supreme moment, would attempt to suggest that his call was unthinking and
without significance. But, gentlemen, I shall prove
to you that such was the foolish, self-convicting custom of the defendant. With the greatest reluctance,
and the—er—greatest pain, I succeeded in wresting
from the maidenly modesty of my fair client the innocent confession that the defendant had induced her
to correspond with him in these methods. Picture to
yourself, gentlemen, the lonely moonlight road beside
the widow's humble cottage. It is a beautiful night,
sanctified to the affections, and the innocent girl is
leaning from her casement. Presently there appears
upon the road a slinking, stealthy figure, the defendant
on his way to church. True to the instruction she has
received from him, her lips part in the musical utterance" (the Colonel lowered his voice in a faint falsetto,
presumably in fond imitation of his fair client),
" 'Keeree!' Instantly the night becomes resonant with
the impassioned reply" (the Colonel here lifted his

voice in stentorian tones), " 'Keerow.' Again, as he passes, rises the soft 'Keeree'; again, as his form is lost in the distance, comes back the deep "Keerow.' "

A burst of laughter, long, loud, and irrepressible, struck the whole court-room, and before the Judge could lift his half-composed face and take his handkerchief from his mouth, a faint "Keeree" from some unrecognized obscurity of the court-room was followed by a loud "Keerow" from some opposite locality. "The Sheriff will clear the court," said the Judge sternly; but, alas! as the embarrassed and choking officials rushed hither and thither, a soft "Keeree" from the spectators at the window, *outside* the court-house, was answered by a loud chorus of "Keerows" from the opposite windows, filled with onlookers. Again the laughter arose everywhere,—even the fair plaintiff herself sat convulsed behind her handkerchief.

The figure of Colonel Starbottle alone remained erect—white and rigid. And then the Judge, looking up, saw—what no one else in the court had seen—that the Colonel was sincere and in earnest; that what he had conceived to be the pleader's most perfect acting and most elaborate irony were the deep, serious, mirthless *convictions* of a man without the least sense of humor. There was the respect of this conviction in the Judge's voice as he said to him gently, "You may proceed, Colonel Starbottle."

"I thank Your Honor," said the Colonel slowly, "for recognizing and doing all in your power to prevent an interruption that, during my thirty years' experience at the bar, I have never been subjected to without the privilege of holding the instigators thereof responsible—*personally* responsible. It is possibly my fault that I have failed, oratorically, to convey to the gentlemen of the jury the full force and significance of the defendant's signals. I am aware that my voice is singularly deficient in producing either the dulcet tones of my fair client or the impassioned vehemence of the defendant's response. I will," continued the Colonel, with a fatigued but blind fatuity that ignored the hurriedly knit brows and warning eye of the Judge, "try again. The note uttered by my client" (lowering his voice to the faintest of falsettos) "was 'Keeree'; the response was 'Keerowow.'" And the Colonel's voice fairly shook the dome above him.

Another uproar of laughter followed this apparently audacious repetition, but was interrupted by an unlooked-for incident. The defendant rose abruptly, and tearing himself away from the withholding hand and pleading protestations of his counsel, absolutely fled from the court-room, his appearance outside being recognized by a prolonged "Kee-row" from the bystanders, which again and again followed him in the distance.

In the momentary silence which followed, the Colonel's voice was heard saying, "We rest here, Your Honor," and he sat down. No less white, but more agitated, was the face of the defendant's counsel, who instantly rose.

"For some unexplained reason; Your Honor, my client desires to suspend further proceedings, with a view to effect a peaceable compromise with the plaintiff. As he is a man of wealth and position, he is able and willing to pay liberally for that privilege. While I, as his counsel, am still convinced of his legal irresponsibility, as he has chosen publicly to abandon his rights here, I can only ask Your Honor's permission to suspend further proceedings until I can confer with Colonel Starbottle."

"As far as I can follow the pleadings," said the Judge gravely, "the case seems to be hardly one for litigation, and I approve of the defendant's course, while I strongly urge the plaintiff to accept it."

Colonel Starbottle bent over his fair client. Presently he rose, unchanged in look or demeanor. "I yield, Your Honor, to the wishes of my client, and—er—lady. We accept."

Before the court adjourned that day it was known throughout the town that Adoniram K. Hotchkiss had compromised the suit for four thousand dollars and costs.

Colonel Starbottle had so far recovered his equanimity as to strut jauntily towards his office, where he was to meet his fair client. He was surprised, however, to find her already there, and in company with a somewhat sheepish-looking young man—a stranger. If the Colonel had any disappointment in meeting a third party to the interview, his old-fashioned courtesy did not permit him to show it. He bowed graciously, and politely motioned them each to a seat.

"I reckoned I'd bring Hiram round with me," said the young lady, lifting her searching eyes, after a pause, to the Colonel's, "though he *was* awful shy, and allowed that you didn't know him from Adam, or even suspect his existence. But I said, 'That's just where you slip up, Hiram; a pow'ful man like the Colonel knows everything—and I've seen it in his eye.' Lordy!" she continued, with a laugh, leaning forward over her parasol, as her eyes again sought the Colonel's, "don't you remember when you asked me if I loved that old Hotchkiss, and I told you, 'That's tellin',' and you looked at me—Lordy! I knew *then* you suspected there was a Hiram *somewhere,* as good as if I'd told you. Now you jest get up, Hiram, and give the Colonel a good handshake. For if it wasn't for *him* and *his* searchin' ways, and *his* awful power of language, I wouldn't hev got that four thousand dollars out o' that flirty fool Hotchkiss—enough to buy a farm, so as you and me could get married! That's what you owe to *him.* Don't stand there like a stuck fool starin' at him. He won't eat you—though he's killed many a better man. Come, have *I* got to do *all* the kissin'?"

It is of record that the Colonel bowed so courteously and so profoundly that he managed not merely to evade the proffered hand of the shy Hiram, but to only lightly touch the franker and more impulsive finger-tips of the gentle Zaidee. "I—er—offer my sincerest congratulations—though I think you—er—overestimate—my—er—powers of penetration. Unfortunately, a pressing engagement, which may oblige me also to leave town to-night, forbids my saying more. I have—er—left the—er—business settlement of this—er—case in the hands of the lawyers who do my office work, and who will show you every attention. And now let me wish you a very good afternoon."

Nevertheless, the Colonel returned to his private room, and it was nearly twilight when the faithful Jim entered, to find him sitting meditatively before his desk. " 'Fo' God! Kernel, I hope dey ain't nuffin de matter, but you's lookin' mighty solemn! I ain't seen you look dat way, Kernel, since de day pooh Massa Stryker was fetched home shot froo de head."

"Hand me down the whiskey, Jim," said the Colonel, rising slowly.

The Negro flew to the closet joyfully, and brought out the bottle. The Colonel poured out a glass of the spirit and drank it with his old deliberation.

"You're quite right, Jim," he said, putting down his glass, "but I'm—er—getting old—and—somehow—I am missing poor Stryker damnably!"

THIS volume is intended to include those selections from the voluminous writings of Bret Harte that best represent the author's characteristic work.

Bret Harte portrayed pioneer frontier life in the West through short stories and sketches that combined dramatic incidents and picturesque scenes with originality, humor and realism. His skillful characterization of individualistic types and a sense of moral contrast won for him a distinguished and lasting place in American literature of the nineteenth century.

To re-create the adventure and romance of a by-gone colorful era in western pioneer life and to acquaint the reader with the most outstanding work of a famous author.

THE EDITORS